Everyman,
and

THE EVERYMAN
LIBRARY

*The Everyman Library was founded by J. M. Dent
in 1906. He chose the name Everyman because he wanted
to make available the best books ever written in every
field to the greatest number of people at the cheapest possible
price. He began with Boswell's 'Life of Johnson';
his one-thousandth title was Aristotle's 'Metaphysics',
by which time sales exceeded forty million.*

*Today Everyman paperbacks remain true to
J. M. Dent's aims and high standards, with a wide range
of titles at affordable prices in editions which address
the needs of today's readers. Each new text is reset to give
a clear, elegant page and to incorporate the latest thinking
and scholarship. Each book carries the pilgrim logo,
the character in 'Everyman', a medieval morality play,
a proud link between Everyman
past and present.*

Alvaro Cunqueiro

MERLIN AND COMPANY

(From the Spanish *Merlín e familia i outras historias*, 1955)

———————

Translated and edited by
COLIN SMITH

Consultant Editor for this Volume
MELVEENA MCKENDRICK

EVERYMAN
J. M. DENT · LONDON
CHARLES E. TUTTLE
VERMONT

Introduction, notes and critical apparatus
© J. M. Dent 1996

Translation © Colin Smith 1996

First published in Everyman Paperbacks in 1996
All rights reserved

J. M. Dent
Orion Publishing Group
Orion House, 5 Upper St Martin's Lane,
London WC2H 9EA
and
Charles E. Tuttle Co., Inc.
28 South Main Street,
Rutland, Vermont 05701, USA

Typeset in Sabon by CentraCet Ltd, Cambridge
Printed in Great Britain by
The Guernsey Press Co. Ltd, Guernsey, C. I.

British Library Cataloguing-in-Publication Data
is available upon request.

ISBN 0 460 87731 3

CONTENTS

NOTE ON THE AUTHOR
AND TRANSLATOR

ALVARO CUNQUEIRO was born in the small cathedral city of Mondoñedo (province of Lugo, Galicia, NW Spain) on 22 December 1911. His father was the town's chemist, whose shop in the main square was a social centre of lively talk, while his mother was specially recalled for her gifts as a story-teller. Alvaro's happy childhood was enriched by the interplay of two languages, his father's Castilian and his mother's Galician. He read History at the University of Santiago and was involved from an early age in literary life, publishing several volumes of verse from 1932, and reading avidly in several languages. After the Spanish Civil War he worked in Madrid as a journalist, lived and wrote in Mondoñedo from 1947 to 1960, and then edited the regional newspaper in Vigo, finding time to travel widely. He died in retirement in Vigo on 28 February 1981.

Cunqueiro is far from forgotten as a poet, or as a fine journalistic essayist, but is best known as a supreme cultivator of artistic but unpedantic prose, full of gentle humour and irony, in narratives with richly imaginative historical settings in both Galician and Castilian. He has been claimed as an unrecognized precursor of Latin-American 'magic realism', but is better regarded as a remaker of ancient myths for modern readers. His reputation was slow to grow and he produced no bestsellers, but he was adored as a writer and as an affable public figure in his native Galicia and had devoted followers elsewhere in Spain. The main titles (in the language in which they first appeared) are: *Merlín e familia i outras historias* (1955), *As crónicas do sochantre* 'Chronicles of the Subcantor' (1956), *Las mocedades de Ulises* 'Ulysses' Youthful Deeds' or 'The Boyhood of Ulysses' (1960), *Un hombre que se parecía a Orestes* 'A Man Who

Looked Like Orestes' (1969), *Si o vello Sinbad volvese ás illas* 'If Old Sinbad Should Return to the Islands' (1961), *Vida y fugas de Fanto Fantini* 'The Life and Escapes of Fanto Fantini' (1972), and *El año del cometa* 'The Year of the Comet' (1974). Of special interest to Britons should be the play *O incerto señor Don Hamlet* 'The Doubting Lord Hamlet' (1959), the product of a lifelong obsession with Shakespeare.

COLIN SMITH was Professor of Spanish at Cambridge until his early retirement in 1990. His main interests are in medieval and Renaissance studies, Spanish language, lexicography, and toponymy, and have recently extended to translation and Galician. He is a Corresponding Member of the Royal Spanish Academy.

CHRONOLOGY OF CUNQUEIRO'S LIFE

Year	Age	Life

1911   Born on 22 December in Mondoñedo, Galicia

1921–7   10–16   Attends *Instituto* (secondary school) in Lugo, Galicia

CHRONOLOGY OF HIS TIMES

Year	Literary Events	Historical Events
1898		Following war with the US, Spain loses her last American possessions: Cuba, Puerto Rico, Philippines
1902		Alfonso XIII (born 1886) crowned
1913	Unamuno, *Del sentimiento trágico de la vida* ('On the Tragic Sense of Life')	
1914–18		Spain neutral during First World War
1916	Foundation of Irmandades da Fala (Society for the Promotion of the [Galician] Language)	
1917	Miró, *El libro de Sigüenza* ('Sigüenza's Book')	
1920	Valle-Inclán, *Divinas palabras* ('Divine Words') Publication of Galician literary journal *Nós*	
1921	Ortega y Gasset, *España invertebrada* ('Spineless Spain')	
1923	Foundation of Seminario de Estudios Galegos (Centre for Galician Studies) Ortega founds *Revista de Occidente*	
1923–9		Dictatorship of General Primo de Rivera
1925	Ortega, *La deshumanización del arte* ('The Dehumanization of Art')	

Year   *Age*   *Life*

1928	16	Matriculates as student of History at University of Santiago de Compostela
1931	19	First work published in a local literary magazine; joins Partido Galeguista
1932	20	Publication of first volume of verse, *Mar ao norde*; several other books of verse follow, and frequent contributions to literary magazines
1936–9	24–7	Works as journalist in the Nationalist zone, living in Ortigueira, Vigo, and San Sebastian

Year	Literary Events	Historical Events
1926–8	J. J. Nunes publishes the collection of the medieval *Cantigas d'amigo dos trovadores galego-portugueses* ('Love-songs of the Galician-Portuguese Troubadours')	
1927	Young poets and critics riotously celebrate the tercentenary of the death of Luis de Góngora, for long a kind of *poète maudit*, the poets (Alberti, Aleixandre, Cernuda, Diego, Guillén, Lorca, Salinas) later becoming known as the 'Generation of 1927'	
1928	Lorca, *Romancero gitano* ('Gipsy Ballads')	
1931	Quincentenary of the death of Villon (to whom Cunqueiro was specially devoted) Unamuno, *San Manuel Bueno, Mártir* ('St Manuel the Good, Martyr')	Municipal elections give victory to Republicans. Abdication of Alfonso XIII; creation of Second Republic
1933	Lorca, *Bodas de sangre* ('Blood Wedding')	
1936	Death of Unamuno (born 1864) and of Valle-Inclán (born 1866); murder of Lorca in Granada	
1936–9		Civil War, resulting in victory by General Franco and his allies. In 1947, Spain was proclaimed a monarchy with regency council and Franco as *Caudillo* (Leader) and head of state
1939	At Franco's victory, many writers, intellectuals, and artists go into exile	

Year	Age	Life
1939–47	27–35	Continues journalistic work for various newspapers and magazines in Madrid (prohibited by the régime from working in this way in 1944)
1940	28	Marries Elvira González-Seco in Mondoñedo
1941	29	His son César born
1944	32	His son Alvaro born
1945	33	Publishes *Balada de las damas del tiempo pasado* (translation of Villon)
1947–60	35–8	Returns to live at Mondoñedo; journalistic work, translations, several minor publications
1955	43	Publishes *Merlín e familia*
1956	44	*As crónicas do sochantre* (Premio Nacional de la Crítica for the Castilian version, 1959)
1959	47	*O incerto señor Don Hamlet*
1960–81	48–69	Residence in Vigo
1960	48	*Las mocedades de Ulises*
1961	49	*Si o vello Sinbad volvese ás illas* ; elected to Royal Galician Academy
1965–70	53–8	Editor of *El Faro de Vigo*, distinguished regional newspaper; publishes many regional guides, books on gastronomy, and collections of short pieces about Galician persons, places, and customs, observations drawn from his reading, etc.

Year	Literary Events	Historical Events
1939–45		Spain neutral during Second World War
1939–75	Franquist censorship of the arts, a little less severe from the mid-1960s onwards	
1942	Cela, *La familia de Pascual Duarte* ('Pascual Duarte's Family')	
1946		Withdrawal of all UN nations' ambassadors to Spain
1950	Delibes, *El camino* ('The Road') Foundation of Editorial Galaxia (publisher of works in Galician) in Vigo	
1951	Cela, *La colmena* ('The Hive')	
1953		Spain makes defence agreement with US, allowing air and naval bases on her territory in return for economic aid
1956	Juan Ramón Jiménez, Nobel Prize for Literature	
1962	Martín Santos, *Tiempo de silencio* ('A Time of Silence')	

Year	Age	Life
1966–8	54–6	Travels to London, Argentina, Venezuela, Brittany, Paris, chiefly as an invited lecturer
1969	57	*Un hombre que se parecía a Orestes* (Premio Nadal); *La cocina cristiana de occidente*
1970	58	Travels to Sweden, Denmark, Switzerland
1972	60	*Vida y fugas de Fanto Fantini*
1974	62	*El año del cometa*
1980	68	Honorary degree from University of Santiago; start of publication of his complete Galician works in four volumes (1980–3)
1981	69	Dies in Vigo, 28 February, after a long illness associated with his diabetes

Year	Literary Events	Historical Events
1966	Delibes, *Cinco horas con Mario* ('Five Hours with Mario') Goytisolo, *Señas de identidad* ('Distinguishing Marks')	
1972	Torrente Ballester, *La saga/fuga de J.B.* ('The Saga/Flight-Fugue of J.B.')	
1975		Death of Franco. Accession of King Juan Carlos I. Removal of most restrictions on free expression
1975–7		Period of 'transition' to democracy. Elections in 1977 place a reforming centre-right government in power
1978	The new Constitution of Spain recognizes the *cooficialidad* (equal official status) of four languages: Castilian, Catalan, Galician, and Basque	
1981		Spain joins NATO
1982		Elections give victory to the Socialist Party (PSOE)
1983		Agreement by which Spain is reconstituted as a state of 17 *autonomías* (regional governments)
1986		Spain joins the European Union
1990		World Cup (Soccer) held in Spain
1992		Olympic Games held in Barcelona

TRANSLATOR'S PREFACE

The translation of *Merlín e familia i outras historias* was
undertaken in response to the organization of a competition by
two bodies of the Xunta (autonomous regional government) of
Galicia – the Secretaría Xeral para as Relacións coas Comuni-
dades Galegas and the Dirección Xeral de Política Lingüística
da Consellería de Educación e Ordenación Universitaria – for
the translation into English of any Galician literary work.
The competition was announced on 17 June 1991 and on
15 November 1991 the panel of judges, consisting of Sr José
Castro, Sr Carlos Durán, Dr David Mackenzie, Prof. Manuel
Míguez, and Dr John Rutherford, awarded the first prize to this
translation, submitted under the code-name *Mister Craven*.
A prize-giving ceremony was held in London on 1 December
1991 during an evening of events organized by the Centro
Galego de Londres. The translator is most grateful to the
Xunta for its initiative, and to the judges, and hopes that his
work will help Galicia and its greatest recent writer, Alvaro
Cunqueiro, to achieve recognition abroad, by introducing readers of English to the special pleasures of Cunqueiro's world of
story-telling. Thanks are offered to John Rutherford for his
careful revision of the translation and numerous suggestions for
its improvement.

The choice of a work by Cunqueiro was a natural one in
1991, for in that year the decade which had passed since the
author's death was marked by events designed to do justice at
last to a writer all too often *marginado* (marginalized) in Spain
outside Galicia and perhaps Catalonia, and scarcely known
abroad. In April the Associaciom Galega da Lingua held a
congress on the writer in Mondoñedo. In May the Academia

Galega invited translations of a poem by Cunqueiro, *Na outra banda* ('On the other side') into a variety of languages, the results being included in a book of essays about the author. On 19 May the Centro Galego de Londres devoted a meeting to Cunqueiro. In August the Universidad del Atlántico of La Coruña organized a course of lectures by distinguished specialists on the writer, and from 9 to 14 September the Xunta acted as patron to the Congreso Alvaro Cunqueiro in Mondoñedo, which gathered over 600 participants from Galicia and the rest of Spain, and from abroad. The proceedings of this have been published (Santiago de Compostela: Xunta de Galicia, 1993). The year also saw the publication of several books and numerous articles on the writer.

The present translator's love of the writer goes back to a year or two after 1955 (date of the publication of *Merlín e familia*), when Reginald Brown, Professor of Spanish at the University of Leeds, returned from Spain with a copy of this attractive novelty and made it known to his colleagues and students. After that it was a case of my acquiring everything of Cunqueiro's that could be found, and eventually of giving lectures (in Cambridge, London, and Antwerp) about his work. In October 1977, thanks to the historian Jaime Ferreiro Alemparte, I – an admirer and already would-be translator – was able to meet the author, and was for several days generously treated as his guest in Santiago, Pontevedra, and Vigo, learning much in conversation with which to enhance and round off the impression formed from reading Cunqueiro's books and studies about him. A few years later the author's ill-health and then his death prevented the realization of a plan to take Cunqueiro on a tour of the south-westerly, that is Celtic, parts of England, and the same in Wales, in the hope that he might give us a book centred upon Cornwall or Dyfed which would form a trilogy with his books which have Brittany and Galicia as their settings (although, on reflection, and as the reader will see, for the British Isles the west of Ireland might have been an even better choice). Yet Cunqueiro travelled largely in the mind, using books as vehicles, and so portrayed

Cornwall and Ireland and many other places without needing to set foot in them.

The paper which the translator presented at Mondoñedo in September 1991 was entitled 'Alvaro Cunqueiro, escritor europeo y universal': an effort to make the Galicians, naturally enough somewhat inward-looking as they struggle to forge and express their newly-freed identity, consider much wider contexts for a writer whose horizons were unlimited in space and in time. It was also urged upon listeners that standard (Castilian) Spanish is less well known abroad than it should be, and that Galician is scarcely known at all, the consequence being that a programme of translation of Galician literature into major languages is essential, whatever the loss – and in Cunqueiro's case it is great – of stylistic savour in the process. *Merlín e familia* returns to the islands of the magician's birth in a language which is not his own but which, one hopes, does not traduce him or Cunqueiro who recorded his deeds.

Merlín e familia is translated from the Galician text, that is the original of 1955, as published by Editorial Galaxia of Vigo in volume II, *Narrativa* (1982), of Cunqueiro's *Obra en galego completa*. As an Appendix there are added texts of the 'Apéndices' from the Castilian version published by Destino of Barcelona in 1969, evidently written as afterthoughts by Cunqueiro between 1955 and 1969: these seem to me to contain materials which are simply too good to disregard, and it can be assumed that if he had lived longer, Cunqueiro would have included them in some new Galician version of the book. Proper names from the Castilian original of these 'Apéndices' have been adjusted to the Galician norms of the main part of the work in order to avoid confusion for the reader.

INTRODUCTION

Galicia, Cunqueiro, and a world of dreams

The *autonomía* (autonomous region) of Galicia in north-west Spain consists of four provinces and has its government established in what was always its spiritual capital, Santiago de Compostela. More than certain other of the seventeen *autonomías* of present-day Spain it has a considerable unity and historical identity: for a few years in the Middle Ages it had its own king, García (1066–73), and before and after that usually enjoyed some form of feudal separateness within the Kingdom of León. Moreover, Galicia has its own language, *galego*, from which Portuguese grew, and a notable literary tradition both medieval and modern. The powerful intrusion of Castilian into many aspects of Galician life, however, from the late Middle Ages onward, had the effect of reducing the language to no more than a rustic patois; in the present efforts to standardize the language and to foster its use in all fields, the example of such writers as Cunqueiro is vital. Galicia claims (with Portugal) a distinctively Celtic character, owed to pre-Roman settlement, but there were Celts in many other parts of the Peninsula, and everywhere Celtic speech was extinguished well within Roman imperial times: the Celticism currently claimed is thus a matter of sentiment but there is no doubting the strength of feeling involved. Audible proof is provided for anyone who hears massed Galician bagpipes, *gaitas*.

Galicia is a land of meadows, hills, woods, streams, and dramatic coastlines with inlets for small harbours on the north coast and spectacular broad estuaries, the famous *rías*, on the west. Rainy and in consequence green, it is to the eye of the

Briton and Irishman, accustomed to the same in the westerly
parts of their islands, the most attractive part of the Peninsula.
It is a land of small farming and fishing communities with the
sort of economy and social arrangements which have led to
overpopulation and then, sadly, in the nineteenth century, to the
mass emigration of its sons and daughters to menial jobs in
cities elsewhere in Spain, to the New World, and in our own
times to industrial work in richer European countries. Attach-
ment to the homeland remains strong, and one finds a Casa
Galega in many of the larger cities of Europe and the Americas.
Cunqueiro travelled far in the imagination but said that his
natural settings, whether notionally of Brittany or Ireland or
classical Greece, were essentially always those of his native
Galicia.

Alvaro Cunqueiro was born on 22 December 1911, the second
of five children, in Mondoñedo in the province of Lugo, today a
cathedral city of some 9000 souls set among hills and woods.
The city has taken to itself, as a kind of civic motto, Cunqueiro's
remark that it is a place 'rich in grain, water, and Latin'. In
different ways his parents gave him much of his essence as a
writer. His mother Pepita, a generous warm-hearted woman
whom her son remembered as 'always smiling', knew ballads
and all the operetta tunes of the day, and was a great story-teller
for the children. His father Joaquín was a *boticario* whose
chemist's shop in the town square was a place of resort for the
locals and a centre of more story-telling, while the torrent of
exotic pharmaceutical names and show of labels on jars
enchanted the young Alvaro and were part of his linguistic
formation. Nothing more natural than that his Merlin should
not be a sinister magician on the grand scale, but a worker of
helpful minor miracles based on recipes written in big books in
strange languages, and an operator of a small furnace in an
outhouse. Joaquín was also a hunter, a very knowledgeable
botanist, as a chemist of the older kind had to be, and a fair
zoologist, who would have educated his son in these matters as

the two of them stepped stealthily through the woods of Mondoñedo. Cunqueiro's story-telling art is evidently developed from his mother's, and many of his materials are just as evidently developed from his father's special loves. There are many tributes more eloquent than anything written on tombstones.

Alvaro went to Lugo for his secondary education and then to university as a student of history at Santiago, but was early involved in politics, journalism, and literary café life. By 1932 it was plain that he was not going to take a university degree (later he remarked that for him and his friends, 'the University of Santiago was in the streets and cafés'), but probably of much greater importance to him, he saw his first book of verse, *Mar ao norde* 'Sea to the North', published, and had for his own satisfaction completed a translation of Villon's work into Galician; Villon's famous *Balade* figures much in his work, he published a Castilian version as *Balada de las damas del tiempo pasado* in Madrid in 1945, and the reader will find *M'sieur Tabarie's Tale* in the present book. (Students who similarly leave without completing their courses may care to note that Alvaro was given an honorary degree by his old university in 1980.) Several other collections of verse followed in the 1930s.

At this time Cunqueiro read a good deal in French (which, with Latin, he would have been taught at school) and evidently acquired a sound reading knowledge of English. His devotion to Shakespeare perhaps exceeded that to any other writer in any language, and was a constant throughout his life. He esteemed Dickens and other English novelists, but confessed an altogether special regard for the Anglo-Irish writer Edward Lord Dunsany (1878–1957). This was probably first stimulated by reading *A Dreamer's Tales* (1910) in the translation published in 1924 as *Cuentos de un sonãdor* in the *Biblioteca* of the prestigious Madrid journal *Revista de Occidente*, edited by the philosopher Ortega y Gasset; afterwards Cunqueiro read Dunsany's other numerous writings in English. He also acquired sufficient German 'with the aid of the dictionary and by hard work and using a certain amount of divination', to translate some of

Hölderlin's poems for a publication in 1950. Among English-language poets he later translated or made free versions of works by Byron, Yeats, Lawrence, Graves, and Pound, and ventured also – probably not from their original languages – upon Kavafis and Pasternak. In Spanish he read avidly and widely, was excited in his youth by the work of the fine poets of the 'Generation of 1927' (especially Alberti), and said that he and his student friends 'had scarcely let a day pass without reading a page or two' of Ramón del Valle-Inclán (a distant relative of Cunqueiro's), especially his four *Sonatas*.

After the disturbances of the Spanish civil war Cunqueiro established himself in Madrid as a journalist and teacher of private classes. From 1947 to 1960 he was resident in Mondoñedo, and was now in a fully productive period in both Galician and Castilian, enjoying at least local esteem as a writer, though probably depending for an income on his journalistic work for newspapers and periodicals. From 1960 he lived in Vigo, eventually becoming editor of the prestigious *El Faro de Vigo*, claimed to be the oldest provincial newspaper of Spain. He loved his journalistic profession despite editorial restraints imposed by commercial considerations and those owed at the time to political censorship. 'I greatly enjoyed the need for improvisation, the speed at which one had to work, the commentaries on the day's events,' he explained late in life when interviewed by a journalist. He was indeed famous for his ability to compose a piece with which to fill a space, not with superficialities but with observations or recollections or tales often good enough to be anthologized and republished later. Many of these are in Cunqueiro's best literary style and contain germs of what could well have become tales or even novels of the kind he did write up and publish, as I have found when sampling – no more than that – a huge range of uncatalogued materials stored in the newspaper archives. His capacity for sure-handed, fluent narration in a singularly engaging style – mostly late at night and sometimes in the midst of a supperless crisis – is astonishing. The participation of creative writers in daily and weekly journalism is

much commoner in Spain than in Britain, but Cunqueiro's ded-
ication and quality were outstanding. After his retirement from
editorship he mused in 1977 that it was not really possible to
compaxinar ('marry, fit together') the two professions, with the
implication that if he had been a less conscientious and hard-
working journalist he might have completed more literary work.
Much of what he produced at this time lies somewhere between
journalism and creative writing: travel guides, provincial guides,
cookbooks, all again of very superior quality. Despite these
other commitments he was in demand as a lecturer and a speaker
at dinners and ceremonies, and was at last able to travel a good
deal in western and Mediterranean countries, even visiting that
Brittany which he had portrayed fictionally years before. This
was in 1968, part of his mission being to sign up bagpipe-players
for a Festival of the Celtic World to be held in Vigo. He also
visited Denmark and Sweden, North Africa, and Buenos Aires.
His connection with Britain was brief and limited to lectures in
London in 1975. After receiving many honours in Galicia in the
late 1970s, Don Alvaro found his activities severely limited by
the sad effects of his diabetes. He died in Vigo on 28 February
1981.

While Cunqueiro in his last years was amply recognized in
Galicia as the finest writer in a remarkable generation of
Galician narrators and poets, and while awareness of this was
crucial to the self-esteem of the emergent *autonomía* and directly
important to its linguistic development, this was not the case in
Madrid or the rest of Spain, except in Catalonia where critics
and readers had shared some of the Galician feelings. Naturally,
when he died, warm tributes and eulogistic, well-informed
surveys of his work appeared in the Spanish national press, but
it was then said that there had sadly been much neglect of the
writer during most of his life. The same is true of another
exceptionally talented Galician novelist, Gonzalo Torrente
Ballester, who only in his late years and partly thanks to the
skilful televising of one of his novels, *Los gozos y las sombras*

'Joys and Shadows', in a series of episodes in 1982, achieved national fame and a wide readership; Torrente had the advantage – from one point of view one has to call it this – that he wrote in Castilian. Much of Torrente's best work involves a kind of fantasy just as Cunqueiro's involves other kinds of fantasy, together with a great deal of gentle, humane humour, and such qualities were clearly not compatible with the vogue for social realism and the social documentary type of novel in the Spain of the 1940s to 1970s. (In 1956 a Spanish reviewer of one of Cunqueiro's books called him 'this noble practitioner of a dead literary genre'.) Even if some kind of 'magic realism' quality can be claimed for Cunqueiro – as it has been for him, and for Torrente too (his *Saga/fuga* was erroneously thought at one time to be a parody of García Márquez's *Cien años de soledad* 'A Hundred Years of Solitude'), he was held to be far outshone by the authors of the great 'boom' of the Latin-American novel of the 1960s and 1970s, and this despite the fact that Cunqueiro's *Merlín* pre-dates these.

The language question was and is a vital one for any Galician writer. Despite the revival of literature in Galician begun by Rosalía de Castro and her contemporaries in the 1860s, major writers of the twentieth century born in Galicia preferred to publish in Castilian, partly because this seemed more natural for them, partly in order to secure a wider readership, and partly because (after 1939) the centralizing policies and rigorous censorship of the Franco years discouraged alternatives (though Galician was not subjected to the same repression as Catalan and Basque, languages of regions which had been Republican in the civil war). It seems certain that such masterly writers as Valle-Inclán, Cela, and Torrente Ballester would not have attained fame and wide readership in anything other than Castilian, although it is some consolation for Galicians to reflect that there is nothing more profoundly Galician in ambience and sentiment than, for example, *Divinas palabras* 'Divine Words' or *La saga/fuga de J.B.* 'The Saga/Flight-Fugue of J.B.' This has of course now changed in the Spain of the seventeen *autonomías*, and for Galicia Cunqueiro and his generation of writers have been instrumental in that change. Even so, Cunqueiro's own attitude was far from constant, understandably in a time of transition. His early prose work was written and published first in Galician, by Galician publishing houses such as Galaxia (a considerable force in regional culture), and a little later was translated by him – sometimes with additions, as in the present case of *Merlín e familia* – and republished in Castilian by houses such as Destino of Barcelona. Later work appeared in either language probably depending on its likely appeal as judged by the author.

Cunqueiro was naturally pressed by interviewers to declare himself on this question, not in terms of cultural politics but as a matter of personal instinct. As is natural enough for anyone of his linguistic make-up, and particularly for someone as word-conscious as he was, he gave different answers at different times. He declared to *El País* on 20 April 1980, 'I don't believe in bilingualism. There is always one language that is basic (*de fondo*) and mine is Galician, but that doesn't mean that I have to translate myself when I write in Castilian. Not at all, since Castilian for me is another language which has the taste of something which is mine as well.' Elsewhere he said he was a bilingual writer 'in the most extreme sense', but a balanced one in whom there always existed the possibility of mutual interferences between languages, to the extent that 'I have to make a certain effort of will in order to stay within one of them in the book or poem I am writing.' It is perhaps an illuminating fact that Cunqueiro as a child spoke Galician to his mother and Castilian to his father (these and other details will be found on pages 21–22 of *Presencia y ausencia de Alvaro Cunqueiro* 'Presence and Absence of A.C.', Elena Quiroga's address on being received into the Royal Spanish Academy on 8 April 1984; printed in Madrid, 1984). The clinching fact is the following: that all Cunqueiro's poetry – surely, with prayer, one of the most intimate of all forms of expression – is in Galician.

The above discussion leads to at least two conclusions of

importance. One is that Cunqueiro, perhaps in our century the finest writer of artistic prose in Castilian, has his bilingual background to thank for that: bilingualism in a writer must surely produce an extra power of words, a special sensitivity to nuances and registers. The other is that Cunqueiro seems to have owed some of that artistry of style in Castilian (the language in which he is best known, if known at all, in Spain generally and abroad) to the qualities of the Galician originals, or to what one might call a sort of Galician mental substratum in cases when there was no Galician original, that is to those 'mutual interferences' mentioned above. Thus one may savour some slight archaism, an unusual form of the verb, a pattern of word-order, a gentle air of linguistic rurality. In Galician and in Castilian, the stylistic vehicle seems perfectly adjusted to the subject-matter. When praised by an interviewer for his style the author replied that he considered himself '*un jardinero del lenguaje*' ('a gardener of language', perhaps 'a careful tiller of the linguistic soil').

This is not the place for a full survey of Cunqueiro's complete work, and as yet no full bibliography exists. To produce one will be a huge task because, as noted earlier, much of his uncatalogued journalistic writing is relevant to his 'literary' production. His poetry in Galician has been neglected outside Galicia, but is of very high quality and has features and tones which link it with his prose writing. Critics have discerned in his verse published in the 1930s the then 'vanguardist' tendencies, variously labelled creationist, imagist, surrealist, and neotrovadoresque. As for drama, the author remarked in an interview that he was strongly drawn towards it and would have written more if there had existed a theatrical tradition in Galicia. We have his remarkable *O incerto señor Don Hamlet* ('The Doubting Lord Hamlet', 1959; second edition, with an additional scene, 1974) which has been played a number of times in Galicia, a lyrical and contemplative piece in which the Shakespearian situation is explored anew on an Oedipal basis.

Cunqueiro was appalled when critics suggested that he was iconoclastically trying to correct or rewrite Shakespeare; we might say that he was rather trying to respond to an obsession which the dramatist had implanted in him from early days. As part of the action of *As crónicas do sochantre*, the strolling players perform a re-creation of *Romeo e Xulieta* in four scenes (and might have continued into more had not a gust of wind torn the back curtain away).

Seven principal titles suffice to give an idea of Cunqueiro's prose narrative. The earliest, *Merlín*, is discussed below. This was followed by *As crónicas do sochantre* of 1956 (*Las crónicas del sochantre*, 1959: awarded the Premio de la Crítica), in which the souls of persons executed for crimes of passion in Brittany in French Revolutionary times, and condemned to wander for a year before final repose, tell their grisly tales. *Las mocedades de Ulises* ('Ulysses' Youthful Deeds' or 'The Boyhood of Ulysses') of 1960 and *Un hombre que se parecía a Orestes* of 1969 ('A Man Who Looked Like Orestes': awarded the Premio Nadal) are re-creations of aspects of classical heroic myth; *Si o vello Sinbad volvese ás illas* ('If Old Sinbad Should Return to the Islands' – in Castilian, *Cuando el viejo Sinbad vuelva a las islas*) of 1961 has the old sailor fantasizing about exploits in oriental seas. In 1972 Cunqueiro published *Vida y fugas de Fanto Fantini della Gherardesca* ('The Life and Escapes of F. F. d. G.'), set in the springtime of Renaissance Italy. Finally – and it has a strong sense of finality about it – there came in 1974 *El año del cometa* ('The Year of the Comet'). To earlier titles it seems proper to apply the description 'narration' or 'prose narrative', but this work is by any definition a novel. A town set in an indeterminate place (sub-alpine France or north Italy?) and variable time, its inhabitants – its very protagonist, Paulos – are dreamed into existence and given a rich life steeped in history, myth, love, and eventually danger. To combat this Paulos enlists the aid of King David, Julius Caesar, and King Arthur, but Paulos's power of dreaming falters and his city, like his own oneiric life, collapses into nothingness. Since Cunqueiro insisted on the power of the imagination and the dream to sustain life, in Paulos's death he was predictively writing his own.

Some critics concerned to define literary trends and schools and to attach neat labels have linked Cunqueiro into the 'magic realist' school of his times, whose creation – with whatever antecedents going way back in literary history – was indeed the work of Latin-American writers in Spanish. This is unsatisfactory and largely erroneous. He was concerned to recreate for modern readers a variety of ancient myths and settings in a series of very personal perceptions. He repeatedly said that they resulted from a sort of disciplined day-dreaming or imagining of the kind which enriches life or indeed without which our life is impoverished and meaningless. The experience of listening to tales as a child and, a little later, of reading tales for oneself, provides the basis for a never-ending process which the eventually disciplined or consciously directed adult imagination, equipped now with confidence and a breadth of reading experience and a style of expression and a sense of literary structures, will express, partly for the satisfaction of the author (that obsession with Shakespearian themes comes to mind), partly to stimulate and enrich readers. The word 'fantasy' has been used above, but any association with the twee world of faerie or the technical extravagances and pseudocosmology of sci-fi is wholly out of place.

The settings and themes chosen for Cunqueiro's fiction coincide happily with very generalized experiences of western mankind in myth-making and in literary tradition: Celtic (Merlin, Arthur, Ireland in a variety of aspects, Brittany as a land of ghosts); classical (Ulysses, Orestes); the fresh new innocence of the Renaissance; even oriental (Sinbad). None of this is romanticized or falsely archaized or viewed with starry-eyed ingenuousness, but is shot through with an entirely modern sense of regretful powerlessness and humorously expressed distrust: Orestes never secures his vengeance but fades away in a mist of self-doubt; King Arthur suffers from an awkward, debilitating, and thoroughly unheroic complaint; Sinbad is an agreeable liar; Fanto dies bereft of his triumphs; and, most tellingly of all, Paulos cannot sustain his dream. There is inadequacy, frailty, defeat, the perpetual sadness of the human condition (alleviated where possible by rueful good humour) everywhere. This gives an answer to those critics who, when not concerned with 'magic realism', have classed Cunqueiro as a writer of '*literatura de evasión*', escapist literature of the kind which in a dull world might provide an hour's diversion.

In *Merlín e familia* as in *As crónicas do sochantre* Cunqueiro sets himself within one of the most ancient literary traditions of western peoples and indeed of oriental ones too: that of story-telling within a framework. From India and Persia the mode spread (as chess did at the same time) into the Muslim empire in Arabic, and thence into Latin and medieval vernaculars. *The Thousand and One Nights*, *The Decameron*, *The Canterbury Tales* and many other collections come readily to mind. In some the framework intrigues the listener or reader as much as any of the tales being told, and in these and others the story-teller emerges as a rich personality. If one feels one knows Alice, Wife of Bath, as well as one's next-door neighbour, and probably remembers her better than the tale she tells, that is a bonus which Chaucer offers. In the same way, Cunqueiro's old boatman who recounts memories of his boyhood and early life – with what embroiderments (fictions within fictions) we can only guess – surely has a full and rounded personality of his own. Cunqueiro himself must have been aware of this because he much extended the old boatman's life in the Appendix he wrote for the later Castilian edition: his creation refused to fall silent the moment his tale-telling function was concluded. Within the fiction – here the best comparision is with *Don Quixote* – the characters appreciate a good story, may comment on the style of the telling, and seem authentically within the now vanished world of the art of the spoken word. Cunqueiro even shows us a professional story-teller, Elimas, giving a virtuoso performance.

As for the geographical setting of *Merlín*, it is identifiably one not far from Mondoñedo. As a boy Cunqueiro went often to stay with relatives in a large house at Riotorto, with balcony, small rooms in the attic, a large yard closed by a big outer gate. This house he calls 'Miranda' and places Merlin in it. Miranda – if Latin neuter plural, 'things-to-be-wondered-at, wonderful things' – is in fact the name of the large surrounding area, still one of the divisions of the diocese of Mondoñedo. Some of what the boy Felipe sees and hears from Merlin's house, especially at night, are doubtless what the boy Alvaro Cunqueiro saw and heard, but others are dreamed and invented, which is why certain unimaginative modern critics are having poor results in trying to track down other Merliny place-names (such as Belvís, Esmelle), personages, and vistas. The eye of the boy-man Cunqueiro bore no resemblance, thank goodness, to the lens of the camera.

Readers of English may at this point understandably have in mind T. H. White's *The Sword in the Stone* of 1938. The comparison is valid but, if it is made, readers will find that Cunqueiro emerges as far superior. White's book (with its continuations much reprinted, of course) enjoyed a triumph with many reviewers and readers, and it enchanted me in earlier days. Today it seems to have some good passages but quickly produces embarrassment with its forced jokiness, pedantic mini-lectures on falconry and tilting and other matters, finger-wagging animadversions to the reader, and ponderous archaisms and technicisms. Cunqueiro's touch is lighter, much more sensitive, the result more coherent and convincing.

In person Alvaro Cunqueiro was large, affable, generous and warm-hearted, greeted wherever he went (as I was able to observe) with respect and great affection. He enjoyed all kinds of company, food and wine (once declaring that any good dish is 'a work of the human imagination'), country rambles, old buildings, his work. He was unashamedly old-fashioned, a traditionalist and monarchist who – as will appear in the stories that follow – would have been happy in almost any kind of non-despotic *ancien régime*, and who indeed lived in many of them in his dreams. He was a sound practising Catholic who reveal-ingly declared to an interviewing journalist soon after Vatican II that he accepted its changes (and greatly liked the Mass in Galician) but that 'Christianity is the religion of symbols and mysteries, and anything which destroys these troubles me deeply'. Perhaps he would like to be remembered as one who cultivated and cherished symbols and mysteries of every kind and wished to share his rich experience of them with his readers.

COLIN SMITH

MERLIN AND COMPANY

CHAPTER I

Remembering

Well, I'm old and tired now; as the years pass there's no fire left any more in the brazier at which I warmed my youthful dreams. I begin to wonder whether those days I spent in my prime in the vast old forest of Esmelle aren't just a lie – a lie I've told myself so often and worked over so many times in my memory that I (the liar) have come to believe I really lived those days, that they really worked dreams and anxieties in me as though there were some magical half-idle carpenter chiselling away in there. True or false, those years of my life or of my imagined life have gone on winding their threads around the spindle of my spirit, and now skein by skein I can weave the fabric of my stories with them.

It was when I was about nine, one Easter, that I went up to my master Merlin's door, clutching my little cap, that little cap which was to be filled for me – who could ever have guessed it then? – with such a wealth of magic, enchantments, inventions, prodigies, transformations, spells. Never, never have such gifts been bestowed upon a child, say I. Now, as though from out of a bottomless horn of plenty, I pull ribbon after ribbon, tale after tale, and with my own eyes I see again all that strange troop of people who came flocking to Merlin, drawn by the fame of his Seven Arts. In Merlin there united, like threads drawn together by some invisible tailor, all the pathways that lead to and come from the world that lies beyond; and he, Merlin the master-tailor, knotted them in whatever way they asked. As you will see.

CHAPTER 2

The Forest of Esmelle

Now this forest of Esmelle, which lies over to the right as you come into the kingdom from León, is probably easier to paint than to describe in words. The road I had followed as far as the Trobos meadow then plunges into the woodland, going up turn upon turn through the tangled thickets of Eirís. After that it follows the river-bank, and when it comes out again on the flat ground, at Paradas, it wanders among muddy pools as far as the place they call Pontigo, which is a low wooden bridge where it's good to listen to the music of the horses' hooves as they go clattering quickly across on their way to Belvís. The mills at Pontigo nowadays are just two dark ruins of blackened stone all covered in ivy, but I can remember the time when they ground wheat from the valleys and rye from the hillsides, and there were apple-trees all along the mill-races: the wind shook the apples off into the water, and there were always a dozen, green and red, dancing on the thick yellowish foam against the bars of the sluices. There's always a wind blowing through the dark oak-wood at Mouras, and the road makes haste to get out of it and emerge into the open countryside of Miranda with its broad ploughlands and fallow patches and pastures over towards El Rei ... From Miranda you can see Esmelle all around you, Belvís castle, the Serpe thickets, Os Cabos lake, and next to it by day the smoke as it rises from the Vilar smithies. At night I used to watch from Miranda as the lights of Belvís began to show in the handsome tall towers, the lights of Vilar making a contrast with them, as though they were set on the ground. When the wind blew from Meira, I stayed still to listen to the strokes of the blacksmiths' hammers. From Miranda you could see over the whole Quintás plain as far as O Castro, and the rye-fields waving like the sea as they answered the touch of the breeze, and the women as they came and went at the Couso fountain. There was a hedge of Roman laurel round the vegetable garden I shall never forget, full of birds whose nests I was keeping an eye on, and just under the house, next to the big straw-loft, there was a lushly sprawling fig-tree. Miranda was Don Merlin's house.

I slept way up in the attic, in a narrow little room with a window right over my bed. At nightfall I liked to climb up on to the bed and look out, staying there sometimes for up to an hour. What fascinated me was the lights. Everything in Esmelle was done at night with lamps. I'm not thinking of the lights of Belvís, which I could watch as they went up and down, like fluttering birds aflame, as they showed in the windows of the two towers; sometimes the whole of Belvís was in darkness, and then you would see a tiny light, like an owl's eye, appear at the balcony over the main door, and I would watch that light go from room to room, brightening for a moment and winking at a window or through one of the arrow-slits, finally appearing suddenly and making signals on the topmost battlements. I knew it was the castle dwarf with his lantern, making his last round. I'm not thinking either of the lights of Vilar, playing among the branches of the birch-trees. The ones I remember best are the lights which travelled the roads, on the highway coming from Meira, and the Quintás road, and the old track which disappears into Os Cabos lake, and the one which skirts the water. Those lights ran along and passed each other, and every so often three or four came together and seemed to make a little bonfire out there in the heart of the night. You could tell they were being carried by horses at full gallop, so quickly did the lights go. And if some light took the Miranda road and came my way, and even seemed – so fast did it come – to be whistling, I felt a stab of fear, like a pin going into a pincushion, and still fully dressed I jumped into bed and pulled the blanket up over my head. It was a blanket with green stripes, and had the name DAVID stitched on to it on both sides, in big red letters. I had claimed DAVID as my protector, and I even prayed to him sometimes. Now that I come to think of it, those stabs of apprehension were a pleasure, really. At dawn – still making a part of my dreams – I could hear the bells of Quintás and the cooing of the pigeons on the edge of the roof. One morning early, at harvest-time, I saw the old sailing-ship on the lake, and another morning, in the autumn, on top of O Castro, I saw the beam of gold. Winter in Esmelle is a long, long business, and except that one moon may bring us frost, it's all rain and snow. Summer is very gentle, though, and autumn too.

Sometimes, to cheer everybody up, Merlin would go out to the kitchen garden, and pour two or three drops of the liquid he called 'of all countries' into a glass cup full of water; then, with a smile – that special open smile which filled his whole broad face in the way the sun fills the morning – he would ask us what colour we would like to see the world. Whenever it was my turn to answer I said blue; then Merlin would throw the water up in the air, and for a second the whole world – Esmelle complete, the white towers of Belvís, the pigeons, Ney the dog, Manoeliña's red hair, my master's white beard, the dapple-grey horse, the Quintás birches, the gorse on top of O Castro – everything was a huge blue cloud which vanished away bit by bit. Merlin smiled as he dried the glass with his black handkerchief. Esmelle, deep old forest, is all tinged with blue in my memory, as if some vast warm moon had suddenly settled on the earth.

CHAPTER 3

Merlin's House

Merlin, as the history books say, was born in a far country, and his mother wasn't married. He inherited Miranda through a sort of aunt on his mother's side, but all this had been so long ago that nobody could clearly recall the details any more. One old serving-woman at Quintás did vaguely remember, though, that when she was a little girl she was taken to the funeral of a lady at Miranda, and Merlin walked in black, with his big red scarf round his neck, behind the priest from Reigosa, who had a splendid singing voice; and even then, Merlin's beard was white. The old woman remembered too that the Count of Belvís was at the funeral with his plumed hat and a dwarf to carry his train, and that women from Lugo had been hired as mourners, and the youngest of them went barefoot and bare-legged. The passing of the years seemed to have no effect on Merlin, and he complained about this as though it were a curse; but this didn't happen often, and he was normally cheerful and open, content with the world, always ready to talk and to offer his friendly smile. He was helped in this by his bright eyes and his lofty, lordly brow, and by the habit he had of stroking his forehead with his right hand when he talked to you. He didn't carry much flesh, but he was nicely built and neat in his appearance, and a great walker. But I wasn't intending to describe Merlin. I had been intending to do a roll-call of his household at the time I lived in Miranda, acting as page-boy and factotum, all for eleven crowns a year and my keep, shoes being provided and patches for jacket and breeches, and also four pairs of stockings every New Year, two white and two black.

The one that ruled the household, that is after Merlin, was my mistress Lady Guinevere. She was a placid person, winter and

summer in her little cloak with beads all round the hem. She was
not originally from these parts either, and seemed to have a
slight speech defect. She had the loveliest long fair hair which
she gathered up into a big bun, and the very whitest skin you
ever saw. She was tall and on the plump side, with a dignified
carriage, and very considerate by nature when giving orders,
though she could be a bit sharp and even curt at times; very
good at keeping people as well as animals in order. She hardly
left the house, and in the afternoons she used to sit in the
drawing-room, next to the big balcony, doing her embroidery
on a big cloth which she wound little by little around a silver
rod. In winter she wore woollen mittens, and white cotton ones
in summer, with little flowers worked all over them. Every so
often she stopped sewing and scratched her back with a boxwood back-scratcher, mounted on a short hazel handle. I think
there was something sad concealed in Lady Guinevere's dark
eyes: if she smiled at you – which was not very often – it was as
though she was begging you to smile too, as a kindly favour.
People said she was the widow of a great king who had died in
war, news of this being brought to her by a crow when she was
on a visit to Miranda, where she was trying out a golden comb.
She was an aristocrat for sure, and Merlin always addressed her
by her title, and she never did anything in the kitchen, except to
prepare a special dish of sweetmeats for some holy day. I think
I can say that she took a liking to me, and on Sundays she used
to iron a white handkerchief for me so that I could blow my
nose properly at Mass. When important visitors came to
Miranda they went up to the drawing-room to kiss her hand,
and Lady Guinevere showed them her embroidery, unrolling it
from the silver rod. I remember that when His Reverence the
Dean of Santiago came to Miranda to buy a pair of nutcrackers,
he put his glasses on to inspect the embroidery, commenting to
my mistress that Tristan seemed a very true likeness, while Isolde
was so lifelike she seemed about to speak. I was waiting at the
door of the room for permission to go in and offer His Reverence
a glass of Getafe wine and sponge-cake with curly edges.

Most of the work in the house was overseen by Marcelina, the matron. She was about forty, short and dumpy, red-faced, terribly talkative, and considered an excellent cook. She looked after everything: the housework, the livestock both large and small, the servants, the farm work, the marketing of the produce, the money side. She adored any novelty, and if some young gentleman came to call, even a Moor, she fell in love with him and remained so for a month. People thought she was in some way related to Merlin, and a niece of the public notary at Azúmara. What she liked most – that is, after being addressed as 'Doña' Marcelina – was that people should think she was party to the secrets of everybody who came to consult Merlin.

'That gentleman who arrived last night, well, he's a messenger from the King of France, who's worried one of his daughters may miscarry. I knew him at once from his black spurs and the silver key dangling from his belt.'

Marcelina knew it all, all the distinctive signs of the people who came and went, all the seven different interpretations attached to every story. To me she was like a good godmother, to the extent that she would say, just as a joke, that I was always pinching the girls.

Then there was Xosé do Cairo to look after Turpin the horse, Ney and Norés the dogs; to go on errands to Meira; to graft the cherry-trees and to keep an account of the labourers who came to do casual jobs. He was a very tall fellow, a bit round-shouldered, with curly hair, small bright eyes, always playing tricks on people. What was surprising in such a well-set-up man were his small ladylike hands, but they made him clever at doing repairs, and he was mad keen on hunting. Since he so liked playing tricks, he didn't have many real friends, but he had guts, and he wasn't bothered about going to Lugo on the darkest night, cutting across the wild land of Eirís, where every day you could hear the wolves howling at people as they went by. Ney the dog slept at the foot of his bed, and Xosé began to treat me in a friendly way when Norés, our otter-hound, who was pitch-black except for his white hind legs that made him look so odd, got into the habit of coming to sleep in my room. The dog could be bad-tempered with strangers, but was always well-behaved with the household. I used to fall asleep to the regular rocking sound of his snoring. Xosé do Cairo, when not playing tricks, was a silent man. On holy days he dined at our master's table, and it was an effort for him to doff his cap to a passing priest.

Then there was Manoeliña de Calros, with her red hair and tiny mouth, her lips tasting warm as milk drunk straight from the cow. She worked in the kitchen and did general household duties. And Casilda, who at one time looked after the blind man at Outes, and now looked after our livestock and the kitchen garden. Finally, there was me, directly under Merlin's orders.

The house stood in the upper part of Miranda, and was large and elegantly built. It had a balcony looking out over the Meira road and a gallery facing south to catch the sun. At the side of the house was my master's workshop, with two more rooms, and beyond that was a stable for visitors' horses; it was my job to look after that, both for regular maintenance and for stabling the mares and stallions. Merlin received his visitors in the big room which contained his furnace, sitting in his green plush armchair reading history tomes on his book-rest. His stag-beetle whistled away in its glass cage, and the scented red liquid dripped from the flask of Fierabras's balsam down the twig of golden Monterroso boxwood into its silver cup. I had to stand next to the book-rest, holding up the candlestick in which there burned a candle made from wax from the Belvís hives, following Merlin's finger with my eye as it traced its way across the pages of his secret books, line by line, spelling out the wonders of the world. Cerís, the blind albino cat, used to come and lie at my feet.

CHAPTER 4

Parasols and Paradarks

I was sitting in the broad shade of the fig-tree, using my pocket-knife to carve a bird on the top of a piece of alder-wood which I was going to use as a walking-stick – I was good at birds, with wings folded and head half-turned – when I heard the four of them riding up. They were all dressed the same: big red hats, yellow capes like those the priests wear at Mass, short leggings split down the sides, and short cloaks round their necks streaming back in the wind, the same colour as their hats. The last horseman led a mule which was carrying the baggage. The party made a grand sight as they came up the slope to the gate of the yard. I ran to fetch my new cap, the one I hung up on the main beam by Merlin's furnace; I'd been ordered to put it on whenever visitors arrived so that I could go and meet them at the gate and take it off as I bowed to them. I'd been well trained in that: the instruction was that I should open the gate with my left hand, and take my cap off with my right, throwing my arm back a bit as I did so, and bending my head just a little. It was a courtesy which my mistress Lady Guinevere had taught me. So I opened the gate to the mounted visitors, and bowed, and the rider who came in first – a fat, red-faced man who had his hat pushed back to reveal a curly wig – asked me where Merlin was. I told him that he was taking his mid-morning refreshment. He explained that they had come from Paris on a very important errand. I left them dismounting and ran to call out to my master, who as usual was eating his scrambled eggs with a sip of rosé wine. Marcelina was already on the scene, I suppose because she'd noticed what a handsome fellow the young man in charge of the baggage mule was, and she came out into the corridor to whisper to me, 'They're Church people: no swords, you see.'

My master was not to be hurried when eating, and insisted on hygiene, washing his hands both before he sat down and after he rose from table. So he took his time in the usual way, washed his mouth out with a last drink of wine, folded his napkin using that special rabbit-ears knot he always made, put on his gloves and his cap with the tassel, and with his hand on my shoulder went out in a formal sort of procession to greet the newcomers.

The four of them bowed very low to Merlin, taking their hats off, and the fat man with the wig spoke very fast in his own language. Merlin listened intently, and while the visitor was speaking he raised his hand two or three times to his cap in the way one does when someone says 'Our Lord God' or 'Blessed Virgin Mary'. Merlin answered him briefly in the same language, and then asked the visitors to go into his furnace-room, that is except for the lad with the mule, who helped me get the horses into the stable and give them something to eat. Then I helped him get the baggage down off the mule; it was quite light, bulky rather than heavy. I made signs to him to say that he could join the others in the house, while I stayed to look after the baggage, but he smiled – and I must say that he was very young and there was something very cheerfully attractive about him, and he was extremely well-mannered – and said to me in Galician:

'No, my friend, I'm afraid I can't leave you in charge of this, because I've been specially ordered to stick as close to it as a nun does to her beads. We've come from Paris in four days – we're from the household of the Bishop of Paris – and what I'd really like from you now is a glass of cold water.'

I went to get it for him from the old well – its water is as cold as snow – and he drank it slowly, enjoying every drop.

'I knew already you were Church people,' I told him when he'd finished drinking, adding that the senior servant in the house had said so, because they weren't carrying swords.

'That senior servant of yours was right in part, but not altogether.'

The lad from Paris lifted a corner of his cape and showed me two ceremonial pistols with decorated silver butts stuck in his belt.

'When you're on the road', he said, 'and you're on a mission as important as the one we're on now, it's no good trusting to charity. Especially nowadays.'

We were chatting away like this when Merlin appeared at the door of his furnace-room and ordered the baggage to be brought in. The lad and I carried it in and put it down where Merlin indicated, on the big table. I was surprised to find that they had lit all the lamps, and that Merlin was wearing his little satin cape across his shoulders. The three strangers were sitting on the bench under the window, the man with the wig in the middle, and it all seemed as though a very solemn Mass was about to start. The packages were carefully wrapped up and secured by seven pieces of string, and when they were opened three large umbrellas appeared, one white, one yellow, one crimson. Merlin picked each one up and kissed its handle, ebony for the white umbrella, silver for the yellow one, gold for the crimson one.

'What splendid parasols,' said my master. 'I doubt if the Pope in Rome has better ones. What your Bishop is asking me to do with them is easy, and I'll do it in a brace of shakes. The white one, as you know, is called "Sun-come-out", and when you open it on the day of the Assumption of Our Lady in August, even if it's rainy at the time, you have a guaranteed sunny morning for the procession. The yellow one is called "Marvels", and it's a mighty secret gadget: you use it only at Whitsun, and when your Bishop is under it, he can speak and understand any language, and even a dumb person can make his confession under it, and your Bishop can hear him. As for the crimson one, well, that's used when you travel by night, and when you open it even on the darkest night you can see as if it were day. It's not really a parasol, more of a paradark, and its name is "Morning Star". When this last one belonged to Lancelot of the Lake, I fixed two of the ribs for him when they came adrift, but I didn't get it quite right the first time, and instead of helping you to see as if it were day, you couldn't see anything at all, not even lighted lamps at night. All the cunning craft of these parasols and paradarks is in the ribs, you know.'

So, while I was serving some wine and ham to the visitors, my master worked on the umbrellas, as skilfully as if he had been an umbrella-mender from Ourense. It didn't take him long: just a question of one rib that was a bit weak, and another that had got detached, he said. Merlin opened and closed them, mumbled some charm or other, smiled, and said in a highly authoritative voice to the man in the wig, 'Monsieur Castel: tell your Bishop that I won't charge him anything for the repairs, but next Whitsun, when he opens the yellow umbrella, he's to pay special attention to the language of magic, particularly the names of the metals and precious essences, because I want to finish reading one of the books about the occult sciences that I have here, one that contains all the lore of the Chaldeans. And tell him not to waste the powers that "Morning Star" has by going to look for buried treasure in caves and holes, because this umbrella was not made for that; it was made so that its owner can follow the steps of Jesus Christ our Lord, by night, along the road to Emmaeus.'

Monsieur Castel stood up and bowed very low. They tied the package up again, and I went with them, cap in hand, as they took their departure and went out through the gate. My master stood at the door of his furnace-room but did not take his cap off to them. The lad who was leading the mule saw that I had jumped up into the fig-tree to watch them as they went off down the hill, and waved to me twice.

'His name is Xazmin', Marcelina told me that evening. 'If I wished, he'd come back for me; while you were giving him his glass of water, he couldn't take his eyes off me.'

CHAPTER 5

The Lay-It-Down-Pick-It-Up-Route

'That lad you see asleep over there, worn out with travelling all the way on foot from the East – it's dusty nearly all the way, and you have the sun right overhead – does in the Emperor of Constantinople's household very much what you do here. That being so, you can address him in familiar terms when he wakes up, and he can teach you some of the fine ways that are in fashion over there. And when you get a bit older, you can let your beard grow too, and if yours comes out as black and curly as his, well, upon my word, it'll suit you jolly well.'

My master said this just as a joke, since I was only twelve at the time; although I was getting quite tall, I still had a child's roundish face, and never a sign of fuzz on it. I went red, as happened for no reason at all when I was that age. Merlin lit the little copper spirit-stove and put the mandrake water on to boil. You'll know that for this plant to keep its powers it has to be picked out in the field under the gallows on which the King's justice has been carried out. Xosé do Cairo brought the last mandrakes in, from Mondoñedo, after they'd hanged Luxilde, the one who killed the priest at Santa Cruz by stuffing rags into his mouth with a cart-staff.

'The worst thing that can happen to an Emperor when he's getting old is to fall in love with a young girl,' my master observed, while he was waiting for his brew to boil. 'The Emperor who's ruling now came to the throne because he was adopted by another ruler before him, one who had no sons. He did have a very charming daughter, however, whom he married to the adopted son. The Emperor now ruling is very fond of wars, a man who has spent most of his life on horseback with the army or on the frontier, and this has made him pretty hard-hearted. It so happened that some princely folk of ancient stock in one of the border regions rebelled against him. These were the men of Gazna, infidels and very cruel people, owners of enormous swords and fast horses. They have a tower in which they trace out the whole pattern of the stars with coloured threads on huge carpets, and they cast their auguries by this. When they saw that Venus was going to pass very close to the Hunting Dogs, the moment for them to enlarge their lands had come. War was declared, and Emperor Michaelos fought his way to the very foot of Gazna, burning the palm-trees and blocking up the wells, except that he left one for pilgrims on their way to Jerusalem; then he sent his herald to the Gaznis, telling them they had two hours to pull down their city gates. The Gaznis listened to the herald's message but said nothing. I was told it was a fearsome sight to see them up there on the battlements of the gateway to Asia, the Seven Princes with swords a foot taller than they were, black uncombed beards, white cloaks splashed with blood, each one with a hooded hawk sitting on the mantel-cloth of his left wrist. The Lords of Gazna gathered round a bonfire to consult over what they should do. One of them, who outwardly was a man of iron but inwardly had a very soft heart, said they might try a ruse he had once read about. It had happened among the Greeks. The idea was to send the prettiest of their girls to Emperor Michaelos; he would fall in love with her, which seemed likely enough, since he was now an old man whose only lovers and friends had for many years been his weapons. He didn't know what a featherbed was, and he had always been faithful to his Empress, Theodora, who was getting on a bit now and being partially paralysed spent her time in a wheelchair in her sun gallery, listening to church music. The Gaznis selected a girl of the blood-royal, a real rose. I know how good she looked because I'm friendly with the painter who did her portrait when she was taking music lessons in Alexandria, and I don't know which you might say was her best feature – enormous green eyes, half-closed, smoothest possible skin, tiny mouth and lovely voice, graceful hands on her viol—'

'Little breasts like a pair of greengages, tiny waist you could encircle with the stem of a rose, delicate arms raised when she sings, long legs that make her seem to take off in flight whenever she dances . . . Her entire being is a mysterious phial of perfume, and now that the whole army is wandering lost in the sands, and the Emperor lies as if in a drunken stupor in his red canvas tent, you still won't find a single soldier who'd say he isn't prepared to die for a lady so sweet and gentle and utterly adorable.'

That was the Emperor's page speaking. He'd woken up while my master was talking. He got up from his rest and did his belt up. There was a dagger with a decorated silver scabbard hanging from it. Merlin took the mandrake water off the fire, put the spirit-stove out, sat down in his plush armchair, and said to the page, 'Well now, Leonís, it's a good moment for you to tell us the rest of the story.'

Leonís stroked his beard and came to sit beside me, on the bench under the window. A beam of golden sunlight came in and played on the silver buckles of Merlin's shoes.

'So Lady Caliela – that was her name, and it means "liquid honey" – arrived in our camp, having herself announced by a trumpet as though she were a messenger from the septuplet Princes of Gazna (yes, they really are septuplets, all born at once, as duly certified by the lawyers and supported by the opinion of an old doctor called Avicenna). She came dressed in just a bit of a silk, with her hair falling free, and the only jewellery she wore was a tiny golden bell at the back of her left knee. A shock-wave ran through the whole army, because they, being good Greek Christians, had never before seen a naked woman in the clear light of day. Lady Caliela knelt down three times before reaching Emperor Michaelos. He was standing there clad in the suit of armour they call the Sphinx, because it has one embossed on the breastplate. He took off his right glove and raised aloft the sword which the Emperors of Constantinople inherited from St Paul, shining as bright as a monstrance with the consecrated Host in it. Lady Caliela knelt at the

Emperor's feet. Then she kissed his spurs and the hand which held the sword, and began to address him in Greek, saying that she brought secret dispatches from Gazna, and that she didn't want the great city to be burned down because she had a dovecot and a rose-garden in it, and in order to save these and a little brother of hers who was sick with a fever that suddenly came over him, she would tell the Emperor by what means Gazna could be taken without bloodshed. She added that she nearly died of fright when she thought of the seven septuplet brothers, each of whom wanted to marry her, and how they, in order to resolve the discord between them, had agreed to share her out, a month at a time, allowing her a month to rest after that in her swimming-pool. She said all this in sweet-sounding rhythmic Greek. The Emperor never took his eyes off her, and when she had finished he handed the sacred sword to his chief general, and laid his great hand on her little suffering head, proclaiming, in a very loud voice so that everybody could hear, that Lady Caliela was under the protection of his imperial arm. The band struck up, people shouted "Huzzah!" and the Emperor took Lady Caliela off to his tent. Ah, would that he had never gone into it!'

Leonís used his cap to wipe away a tear, and then as if talking to himself, very quietly and gently, he continued, 'But how could he not have gone in! That sweet and lovely girl carried a fearsome destiny with her. Lady Caliela spent two whole days and two whole nights with the Emperor in his tent, telling him all about the confidential dispatches from Gazna; the secret gate into the city, which they say led into the Jewish quarter; and what would be the best time to attack – at curfew. These were the rumours that were going round. The deadline which had been given to the Gazna rebels went by, and then more days, and then the Emperor appeared with Lady Caliela, on horse-back, and at the gallop they rode round the walls, viewing the lofty towers. People started to say that Lady Caliela had bedded Emperor Michaelos, and that our royal master was so far seduced by her caresses and by the warmth which emanated

from such a female flower that he had forgotten all about
Gazna, the seven septuplet Princes, the war, and his sword.
Then one morning, when the sun was breaking red over the
hills with their peach-trees and their orange-trees, the trumpets
and drums sounded and we struck camp, setting off on a long
march. Within two days we had left behind the fields and the
pools, and we headed out into the desert and drank from the
wells at the oases. They said we were off to attack Pharphistan,
which is where the Gazna people keep their secret treasure,
Lady Caliela having told the Emperor about their mountains of
gold; indeed at night, when we camped in the sand, you could
see the lights of the Pharphistan oases in the distance. Oh, we
saw them many nights in succession, and many mornings too,
those so distant towers of rich cities, standing out on the bright
band of the dawn! But it was all like a huge fraud that someone
was perpetrating with a mirror, and now the great army is
wandering about lost in the sands, hungry and dying of thirst,
and the only one who is happy is the Emperor, because he's got
Lady Caliela's arms around his neck, and those lovely red lips
to quench his thirst . . . What happened was that Lady Caliela
tried to send the Gazni Princes a message to say that when
summer came they should go out to the meadows along the
river and there obliterate, with sword and arrow, all that was
left of the flower of Byzantine military power. The messenger
was I; she gave me a part-payment in gold, and promised me a
favour of my choice when I returned, provided I had delivered
the message. She gave me directions for the journey in a little
silver box with a needle, and when I reached the three hot-
water springs, I was to follow the breeze from the sea, and in
another four days I should be in Gazna and at my ease. I agreed
to all this, but had further instructions from Christophoros the
polemarch, who told me that instead of following the sea-
breezes I should follow the Levantine ones, going by Tripoli of
Antioch and from there in a ship of the Emperor's service to
Marseilles, then along the pilgrims' road to Compostela, and
then in one day more to Miranda. There Merlin, who was a

good friend of his, would lend me that itinerary which he brought out of Brittonia rolled up in an iron tube, known as the Lay-it-down-pick-it-up-route. Then I could start to lay the route down at Aleppo in Syria, and use it the way a flock of swallows does when they fly south in the autumn, all the way to where the brave palace guardsmen and the heavy cavalry and the lancers with their crimson cloaks and the archers with the red crosses on their breasts lie dying, and they could all travel back along it to Constantinople to rebuild the Empire and exorcize that dark deceitful passion out of Emperor Michaelos's body. Such, my lord Merlin – may God and St George protect you! – is my mission, and my heart is breaking when I think of those burning sands, that ceaseless thirst, the endless wandering, and even when I think of Lady Caliela, who promised me a favour.'

'Leonís, I would gladly lend you that itinerary, but it got rusty by being kept in the attic in the iron tube. All it's good for now is four leagues, and it shrank so much when it got soaked as I made my way along it from Galicia to Avalon, to attend Don Amadís's grandchild's wedding, that now it's only as wide as a table-runner, and people can only go in single file along it. So that remedy is no good any more. What I can give you is a thread you'll have to tie to the lemon-tree next to Holy Trinity Church in Aleppo; you throw the ball of thread on the ground, and shout at it "On you go, on you go!" In two days you'll find it leads you across the desert to your people. Then you can bring them back safe and sound. As for Lady Caliela, look for an archer in the Royal Guard who has one red eye: he's to use this eye alone when he takes aim, and shoot her straight through the heart.'

'I know that archer: he's the Prince of Thebes, grandson of a very famous king they called Oedipus.'

Leonís kissed my master's hand, picked up the ball of thread which was well wrapped in a green silk handkerchief and then packed in a carton labelled 'Best Iced Cakes from Astorga', and went off at once at full gallop on his bay horse down the Belvís road. I never was able to hear if he got there in time. But I keep a very clear recollection of Lady Caliela: she comes into my dreams sometimes, slipping into them as easily as you slip a ring on your finger.

CHAPTER 6

The Little Princess Who Wanted To Marry

It was about midsummer, the eve of St John's day. I was watching the dwarf coming up from the castle and finding it amusing to see the tiny fellow on his tall mule of the Meira breed with its calm measured tread like that of a woman pregnant for the first time. When he got closer I could see he was carrying a letter with a seal dangling from it by a green ribbon. This was for my master Merlin. Whenever the dwarf came to Miranda – he was a servant of the Count's – he would go upstairs to greet Lady Guinevere, giving her news of the Count's daughters and of the Countess's little Pekinese (Merlin, by way of a joke, had taught the dog to whistle an aubade). The dwarf was of the limp-wristed persuasion, and liked to talk to my Lady about the latest Parisian modes, and what ribbons were being delivered to young ladies in Venice, and a new perfume called 'frangipani essence', and the latest versions of the waltz, and what marriages were being arranged in the nobility. Lady Guinevere served him meringues, and, if he wasn't in a hurry, he sang a habanera for her that she was very fond of. What most used to annoy me about the dwarf was the lordly tone he adopted with the servants, as if he were not himself a wage-earning page, and he even expected me to hold his mule's head while he mounted. Once, he came with a straw hat – a very fine one, it has to be said, with a great band of pink tulle round it – and I had to put that on for him too, the way you might place a mitre on a bishop's head, and then I had to adjust the band, whose ends came down to near his waist. Anyway, he brought the letter, paid his respects to Lady Guinevere, and went back to the castle on his mule, which looked as conceited as he was. My master was troubled by what he read in the letter, and he called Marcelina and instructed her to prepare a bed with the very best linen in the drawing-room with the balcony.

'With all this fuss', Marcelina said to me, 'I should think we're going to get a visit from some marchioness, or maybe the Princess of Ireland, the one who, according to the papers, is losing her sight day by day. Or it might be a visit from that niece of the Dean of Truro whose hand turned into silver. If it is indeed to be she', said Marcelina, chucking me under the chin, 'you'll be doing well, because these young Truro ladies all fall in love with page-boys, and they think nothing of scattering kisses around. What would people say if I started doing the same!' This made me spend the following days full of expectations about the visit, and I made myself blush imagining it would be the Dean's niece, and that she would favour me with a kiss.

It turned out that when the visitors arrived I was wearing my coat with the elegant trimmings, and my new cap with the pheasant feather sticking out of the top, and well-polished shoes, the reason being that I had just returned from taking a present of trout caught by Xosé do Cairo in the Pontigo mill-stream over to the parish priest of Quintás. There was a knocking at the outer gate, and I ran out of the furnace-room – where I was giving the stag-beetle a meal of flies for its supper – and went to open the gate. It was a gentleman dressed completely in black, with frock-coat and top hat and a golden chain round his neck; he was holding the reins of a roan horse on which was sitting a lady whose face was covered by a thick white veil, and she was all in black too, except for her gloves which were white, and on each glove there was embroidered a red carnation. It was getting dark, and in the shadow of the gate I couldn't see the man's face at all clearly, but he was the tallest man I had ever seen.

'Your master is expecting us,' he said, in a curtly authoritative tone.

I took off my cap and swept him a bow. As they entered the yard Merlin and Lady Guinevere were already at the house door, and although it wasn't properly dark yet – summer twilight in Miranda lasts a long time – Xosé do Cairo was beside them holding his silver lantern at the level of their heads. Merlin and the gentleman clasped each other, the lady in the veil and my mistress embraced, my master kissed the unknown lady's glove, and the gentleman did the same to Lady Guinevere. Then the four went up to the drawing-room, led by Xosé with his lantern. I put the horse in the stable – he seemed very hungry, and was covered in sweat – and all the while I was painting in my mind a portrait of the fantastically lovely lady who had arrived at our gate. But I didn't get a chance to see her that day, because Merlin called me and told me to go and keep watch at the gate, since a servant with a trunk and a wicker cage was expected: as soon as he arrived I was to take the trunk up to the drawing-room with the balcony, and take the cage to the furnace-room, and then send the servant on his way to stay at Belvís castle.

It was after ten o'clock when the servant arrived with the trunk and the cage, and it turned out that I recognized him, from his big red moustache, having met him once when I went to the Meira fair. I said as much to him, and he asked me in a low tone to keep quiet about that, because it was all part of an old story, and it was best that nobody should know he had been in the area before. I said no more, but resolved that I should tell Merlin about it if ever it seemed right to do so. I took the trunk up to the drawing-room, and then stopped for a moment in the passage to see if I could catch what was being said in the other room, but all I could hear was Lady Guinevere's voice telling a tale about Lord Parsifal which I had often heard from her lips. I put the cage in the guest-room as my master had told me to. It was a very well-made cage, of wickerwork painted blue and white, quite big enough for me to get into. At the bottom of it I could see a little velvet cushion. Then I went to have my supper in the kitchen, with Marcelina and the girls. They were all terribly curious, and made bets about whether the veiled lady was young or old.

'She has a young girl's voice', declared Marcelina, 'and an elegant walk.' I chewed on a chestnut and went up to my room, though I didn't feel sleepy; but I counted sheep and eventually dropped off. I couldn't have been asleep for long when Merlin came to call me and tell me to go down without a sound to the furnace, where he needed me. I went down with my shoes in my hand, so as not to make any noise. Merlin was sitting next to the cage, which wasn't empty any more. There was a small creature in it, a sort of little hind or fawn, lying down with her head resting on the cushion. The most startling things about her were her blue eyes and the sad expression in them. Merlin ordered me to bring some milk in a cup, and if it had set a bit in the cool part of the larder, so much the better. I fetched the milk, and Merlin fed the little creature with it in a spoon. While he was doing that I put my hand between the withies and stroked her; she made a grateful low sound in her throat, like old dogs do when you soothe them. My master threw a cloth over the cage, and sat down in his plush chair to look through a book I had never seen him use before: it had a picture of an animal on every page, with such bright colours that it was a delight to look at them. I held up the candle for him to read for a good hour. Then he shut the book and said, 'You'll have to give me a hand tomorrow, Felipe. Don't be afraid, and don't tell anyone you saw the fawn in the cage. It might be that when you come down tomorrow to start cleaning up you won't find her, but don't go asking any questions.'

That was the moment when I thought I should tell my master about the servant with the red moustache. Merlin asked me if I was sure, and I said I was, because I remembered too that Mr Moustache had been eating octopus beside us at the Meira fair, and had paid for it with a peso coin, and the woman who kept the fish-stall, Mistress Benita de Sarria, had called him a cheat, because the coin turned out to be a Sevillian one which was no use in these parts.

'It seems to me, lad, that in any one region you can always find a daemon that looks like another daemon. Now you go off to bed.'

Midsummer, about St John's day, is very beautiful in

Miranda. All the garden walls have cherry-trees beside them, and the white cherries in our kitchen-garden had a sugary-cinnamon taste to them that was a joy to savour. I hadn't slept much with so many mysterious things going on, even though in Merlin's house we were pretty used to odd comings-and-goings. When I went down to start cleaning, the first thing I did was to peep in the cage. It was empty. I shook the cushion, which still carried the impression of the fawn's head, and was still warm to the touch. Then I swept the rooms out, fed the roan horse that belonged to the top-hatted gentleman, caught a few flies in the stable to give to the stag-beetle, dusted the mirror and the plush armchair, stuck a new candle in the candlestick, and topped up the snuff in my master's mother-of-pearl snuffbox, from which Merlin would take a pinch from time to time with two fingers and apply to his nose. Those were my usual daily duties, before breakfast, and breakfast in cherry-time always consisted of cherries and wheaten bread. I was jolly good at spitting the stones out, almost as effective as a catapult shooting dry beans, and I was teaching Manoeliña de Calros to spit them too at the time. That way I could touch her sweet pink face and her lips, and she knew perfectly well that I liked touching her just as much as I liked teaching her to spit cherry-stones. But there wasn't any spitting-class that morning, because Merlin called down to me from the balcony, telling me to chain up the dogs in the outhouse, and get the furnace going with gorse-wood, and then not to move from there even to wet the mops. So I sat down next to the furnace and started cutting a big F on each of my clogs, and then Merlin came in with the gentleman. It emerged that Monsieur was the mayor of a town in France called Bordeaux, and guardian-in-law of the mysterious lady. My master Merlin told me so, introducing me to Don Silvestre as Felipe – well, that's my name – his highly-esteemed page. Don Silvestre greeted me by raising an eyebrow. He was a very solemn sort, clean-shaven as a clergyman might be, and he wore gold-framed spectacles with rather thick lenses. Behind them you could see long bright lights, so that you might have thought he had knives in his eye-sockets rather than pupils. And he was taller than any other man I'd ever seen.

'This lady, Felipe, who came with Don Silvestre, belongs to a great family in the province they call Aquitaine, which spreads out to the right as you cross into France from here. This little Princess wanted to marry a young man of the area, of perfectly good family, but just before they were going to meet for the marriage ceremony, the girl's face began to get covered with black blotches, and then she began to sweat all over, her ears grew and hair started to sprout all over her body, and finally she turned into the fawn you saw in the wicker cage. She's been in this state for nine weeks. By day she's a woman, except that she's covered in hair, and sometimes at night she turns into a hind, as before. What I'm going to do now is prepare to carry out a well-tried operation to break the spell. You'll have to help me; as I said, there's nothing to be frightened of. I expect Don Silvestre will give you a couple of golden guineas as a reward.'

I said that of course I was glad to help, and I felt very proud at so much confidence being shown in me. While I put my clogs on, I was already thinking that with two guineas I'd be able to go to Lugo and buy myself a straw hat with a band like the one the dwarf of Belvís had, and a silver watch with a golden knob to wind it up with, just like Xosé do Cairo's. Don Silvestre said he would go and keep watch over Lady Simona – that was the enchanted lady's name – while I stayed with Merlin. We closed the doors firmly and my master rehearsed the main points of the operation. First he kneaded some dough of wheat flour and made a ring-cake with it, and with some dough left over he made two strips to form a cross on top, which we put in the oven to cook. Next he tied a thread to a wolf-trap, unrolling more than ten yards of it and tying the other end to a little silver bell, on which he then drew four crosses with red ink.

'When you see me make so many crosses on an object', said my master, 'you can be sure it's because we've got some daemon mixed up in the business.'

I think I didn't eat anything at all that day, being so unsettled and on edge. Marcelina tried to pump me for information, but I said nothing, or talked about something else.

I spent the afternoon cleaning out the furnace, and took the dogs out into the woods for an hour to see if they could pick up the scent of a fox that had been coming after our chickens, and put a patch on one of my clogs. Then I had eggs in breadcrumbs for supper, and as soon as it was dark I presented myself to Merlin, as I had been ordered. He was wearing a hunting outfit.

'Now the sort of spell that has been used on Lady Simona', my master explained, 'is the kind people use on Midsummer Eve. They last just a year – they're small-scale enchantments, you might say – and most of them are the work of daemons of the fornicating sect. The daemon who put the spell on her will come back tonight – because it's such a special night – and I've got everything ready so that we can catch him in the act and send him tumbling down the rocks.'

'Couldn't we kill him?' I asked, trying to make out that I would be brave enough to do it myself.

'Either way it won't matter, because for as long as the world lasts, the total number of daemons will always be the same.'

Eleven had struck on that Midsummer Eve when Merlin and I left the house, with yours truly holding the rope with Lady Simona, changed again into a hind, at the other end of it. I said earlier what lovely moist blue eyes she had. Merlin didn't say a word as we set off along the path to the Couso fountain. When we got there he tethered Lady Simona with a plaited thong, and told me to take her out into the meadow to graze. She began to put her nose very calmly down in the grass, just as if she were grazing. It was full moon, shining so bright that you could hardly see the stars around it. The cool water of the Couso fountain sang its tune as it spouted from the high pipe fixed in the angel's mouth. The angel has a plaque in his hands with an inscription that reads: 'I belong to Belbis'. Usually there are bats fluttering round the fountain, but they weren't flying that night.

Nearly an hour went by like that, the two of us sitting beside the fountain and Lady Simona grazing in the meadow, when suddenly my master must have heard something, because he told me to take the hind to feed over by the apple-trees near the churchyard. I took her over that way, and when I got to the apple-trees I spotted the wheaten ring-cake with the cross on top, down there in the grass, but I didn't touch it, because Merlin had forbidden me to touch or mention any of the spell-breaking preparations. Lady Simona was feeling unsettled now, maybe because she wasn't used to being tethered: she insisted on rubbing against me, and I could feel the alarmed beat of her heart on my leg. Then I saw Don Silvestre appear among the apple-trees. Without looking in our direction he went over to where the ring-cake lay in the grass. He seemed taller than ever in the moonlight, and his odd figure was enough to send a shiver up your spine. He began to tear branches off the trees like a madman and pile them up over the ring-cake until he had covered it completely. Then he turned towards us. He wasn't wearing his glasses now, and his face had the look that a wolf has at night. Lady Simona was no longer a hind now, but a girl crying into hands held by the plaited thong. She pressed close against me. Don Silvestre couldn't take a single step: he put his left foot straight into the wolf-trap, whereupon the little silver bell tinkled, and Merlin shouted something in Latin. I ran with Lady Simona beside me towards him for protection, but we slipped in the mud just before we got to the fountain, and I must have fainted . . . When I woke up I was on my bed, and there was Merlin sitting on the chest beside it. He gave me a broad smile.

'So that, my lad, was the daemon. I must say you did very well. Lady Simona is free of the spell and has gone to Belvís, and tomorrow she can start off for France under the protection of the Count; and then she can get married as she wishes. I was sorry you weren't able to see how Don Silvestre, who was not really Don Silvestre at all, but a daemon named Croizás, shot off down the Quintás road looking just like a bundle of straw on fire. Every single dog in Esmelle barked a good hour or more. That Mr Moustache you had met in Meira was Croizás's footman, and he had shut the real Don Silvestre up in an attic so that the daemon could cast a spell over Lady Simona for a second and final time. Well, Croizás will have to go and change his skin in hell. As for Mr Moustache, well, his real name is Tadeo and he was once a tailor in Toledo, and they'll be taking him to France too, where he committed a murder and where the King's hangman is waiting to receive him at Pons. That's a very pretty town, by the way, and they make some decent wine there.'

I didn't say anything, but of course Merlin could read my thoughts, and he said to me in the kindliest tone, 'You'll be wondering about Lady Simona, naturally. She told me to say goodbye for her, and she's left you this embroidered hankie and half an ounce of gold. She wanted to clean your coat with the trimmings, but I said it was best to let the mud dry first. She ran her hand over your hair and said with a laugh, "The mud comes to here on him!" Now you get a bit more sleep, till they call you to go to Mass. You know, you got baptized a second time last night, because at midnight on Midsummer Eve, every seven years like this one, every single fountain in the world runs for a moment with water from the River Jordan, the water that St John used when he baptized our Lord.'

He gave me another smile, and before he went out he took a look at my coat with the trimmings all covered with mud, hanging by the window so that it should dry quicker. Then I remember he said, in that friendly tone which I knew came from his knowledge of people's hearts and of people's dreams and the solitary thoughts each one of us keeps close-guarded in the pocket-book of his soul, 'Jolly handsome you looked when we went off to do our spell-breaking! I found your new cap in the mud by the fountain, but you'll need to stick a different feather in it.'

CHAPTER 7

The Mussulman's Stories

I went around that summer feeling very low, sick with love of Lady Simona. She wasn't there to be seen any more, but I could dream pleasurably of her blue eyes, and, with a sigh, I could catch the scent of her too, when I put to my nose the embroidered handkerchief which she had left me as a present. The local festivities held no charm for me, not even the St Barnaby junketting at Quintás, which is very famous, nor Our Lady's at Meira, nor St Bartholomew's at Belvís . . . So I went around alone and a bit footloose, not concentrating much on my work, especially as Lady Guinevere had gone off to the hot baths at Lugo, taking Manoeliña with her as her maid, and my master had started to read some new books they sent him from Rome. These had been brought by a Mussulman called Elimas: that, it seems, is a name used among his people for magicians, ever since an Elimas had a quarrel with St Paul. He wasn't a Christian, and he didn't touch pork or wine, but on the other hand he liked coffee, and smoked a long decorated pipe all the time. While my master was selecting books to buy, which Elimas had brought in a basket lined with cloth on his Leonese donkey, taking two days over it, I struck up an acquaintance with Elimas. I served him his chocolate drink, and sponge-cake for him to have in bed, and took his donkey to Vilar to be shod, and put new studs on the soles of his boots. What most impressed me about Elimas were his loose-fitting green trousers, and his habit of taking off his shoes when he came into the house.

'I've been all of twenty years', he told me, 'travelling about selling secret books, treatises on the alchemical art, talismans, amulets, amber cups, good cheapo spectacles, and I can say I've been all over the nine parts of the world and maybe one or two more on top of that, and I can tell you Miranda here is rather out of my way, but you see I really like your master Merlin a lot; I mean, if it wasn't for him, right now I'd be going into Rome, or just crossing into China, or I'd be in Havana, where I've got a little affair going on.'

Mr Elimas didn't stir his coffee to make the sugar dissolve, but drank the coffee first, and then with a spoon he scooped up the sweet syrup that was left at the bottom of the cup.

'Beyond that', he went on, 'I earn a bit telling stories round the inns. Right now I've got a set of seven, all nicely thought out, all with an element of truth in them. However much you put into a story out of your own head, and even though most of it comes that way, there are always four or five threads of truth in it too, things you might have carried in your memory without realizing it.'

'Well, that's for sure,' said my master who happened to hear this. 'And this very evening you could give us the gist of one of your stories.'

'Certainly, sir,' said the Mussulman, who always treated my master with the utmost respect, 'and I could start on it right away if the lad would be so kind as to bring me another cup of coffee.'

I ran off at once to fetch it, and we all sat down in the broad shade of the fig-tree – Merlin in his rocking-chair, the Mussulman on the ground as is their custom, me with legs astride the big branch. Elimas drank his coffee, took his time over sipping up the sweetness, and began on his stories.

THE DEVIL AND THE BATHTUB

'This happened about a year ago, in the Kingdom of Naples, on the Prato Nuovo estate, which belongs to a not-too-legitimate niece of the Grand Inquisitor. You'll see from the story that not even the top Christian people can keep clear of Old Nick's clutches. Well, this lady, whose name was Donna Eleonora, gave birth to a boy, and they started to bath him in a new glass tub they were using for the first time. The moment they popped the little mite into the water, he dissolved away into nothing, just as if he'd been made of salt or sugar. A great cry of terror filled the whole house, and no-one could credit what had happened, but there was no arguing with the fact that the child had vanished. They poured the bathwater away in the cemetery, and buried the jug in which the water had been carried with full pomp and circumstance, you know, music and responses with lots of grace-notes and the Grand Inquisitor in full canonicals. Now, a fortnight ago the lady gave birth again, and since a new-born baby has to be washed, they again brought out the glass bathtub, which is quite an antique, very valuable. This happened in the lady's bedroom, in the presence of the Grand Inquisitor, and of the exorcist of Palermo, who is the person you have to employ whenever there's a daemon to be chased out of the bodies of the Naples branch of the Bourbons, as tends to happen nearly always in leap-years. The top people of the medical profession of the Two Sicilies were there too. Just as they were about to pop the baby into the water, it occurred to the mother that her "uncle" should bless the bathtub. Hardly had the Grand Inquisitor got the words "*In nomine Patris*" out when the tub shattered into a thousand pieces, there was a terrible stink of sulphur, and the exorcist of Palermo managed to catch the imp round the neck with the curved handle of his umbrella as he was trying to get away. But the daemon got free, and disappeared up the chimney. Later it was discovered that the tub had been bought from the Fossano convent – it's very well known, it being the tub which the abbess used for her bath at Easter-time and Martinmas, and the nuns on St Peter's day – and they learned that it wasn't really a bathtub at all, but a daemon that had changed himself into one, so that he could take a look at the nuns in their birthday suits.'

THE CROWN PRINCE OF CHINA

'The heir to the throne of China, a slightly dim youth, wanted to get married, and his father, against all tradition, allowed him to choose a bride. He was not only rather dim but also in poor health just then, spending his time painting flowers and birds, and every night in his room in the Palace of a Thousand Weathercocks, he dreamed that his hand was caressing round lemons. The Prince ordered that portraits of the loveliest girls should be sent to him from all over the Empire, painted on long strips of silk, and he spent his days gazing at them, without finding a single one to his liking. At night-time he dreamed that his hands were resting on a little basket made of feathers, in which someone had placed two round lemons ... Then from the most remote of all the provinces there arrived a messenger who brought seventy portraits for the Prince, all of young girls depicted smiling as they shyly bowed their charming heads. As the Prince unrolled the scroll with the portraits of the girls, each one having her name and rank embroidered beside her, the Prince suddenly found himself staring at the picture of a girl who raised her face for him, and opened her green eyes with black eyelashes as long as the hairs of the brush with which the Chinese paint the first letter of the name of the Dragon. The two looked long at each other, and then the girl, becoming still again there on the painted silk, blushed. The Prince ordered – this was eleven weeks ago – that she should be brought to him, and she was, and they were married. Now in China marriages take place with a painted paper lantern: the couple wait until the candle has burned away, and the lantern has gone out, and the ceremony is over. The Crown Prince gave his bride two sun-shades, a pearl necklace, a silver shell, and ten ounces of gold. When the formalities were over and the two were alone in their bedroom in the Palace of a Thousand Weathercocks, the Prince asked the girl why she had blushed in the portrait. "Well," said the bride, "those two lemons you fondled in the night-time ... those were me." Then the Prince, who in a short time put on four Cantonese pounds in weight, changed his wife's name on the advice of his court officials, and from then on all documents called the Princess, in those special elegant letters they have, "The Lemon that Smiles in the Night".'

THE WOLF THAT HANGED HIMSELF

'This is a new story about something that happened last winter in the Kingdom of León, in an oakwood called Dueñas, some nine leagues from Astorga. People are singing songs about it already in León and Palencia, but it's not known hereabouts as yet. What happened was that a wolf hanged himself. The story goes that there was an old wolf, of the kind they call "brigands", because they're always prowling round villages and farmsteads and have no fear of man. He caused havoc among the dogs, attacked people, and killed a soldier and a little girl who was taking a donkey out to pasture. He paid special attention to the girls, particularly if it was a certain time of the month with them, and he came to howl at them right under their windows. The village priest and a famous hunter called Don Belianís – he's a half-brother of the Archpriest of Los Vados; he buys books about gunpowder from me, and last year I sold him Biringuccio's *Pyrotechnics* – these two with the men from the Santa Hermandad patrol and the Marquis of Astorga's servants armed with shotguns assembled to hunt him down. Once one of the King's hounds named "Segovia" had picked up the scent they got on the wolf's tracks in the scrubland, and followed him day and night through the hills, and at dawn they had him surrounded in the Dueñas oakwood. This was a triumph for Segovia, but also for the men who had so laboriously followed on. Don Belianís went into the wood with his gun at the ready, and there watched – he still hasn't got over the shock – while a naked man hanged himself from an oak-tree, tying a rope round his neck and then to a branch and letting himself drop, and as he fell, turning into a wolf, the same old wolf as had been causing all the trouble. So it was that people realized the fearsome beast had been a werewolf after all. The priest, a worthy and compassionate man, organized a funeral for him, and as he was saying an "Our Father" over the body – he might have been in time, you never know – while he was still praying, the wolf turned back into a man, and everyone recognized him as Romualdo Nistal, who had kept a shop over in Manzanal: a well-thought-of chap, who never gave short weight.'

'Those, then', said Mr Elimas, 'are the first three tales, and I generally tell them the first night in the inn. Naturally I dress them up a bit, giving details about people: saying that some character was lame, or had made a second marriage with a deaf woman who had money, or had a lawsuit going on about the water supply, things like that. And I add bits about the towns, their size, how many squares and streets they have, what the fairs are like, what the local fashions are. Stories, you know, like women, like dishes, need some decoration. About this Romualdo Nistal, to take him as an example, I might tell about his life when he went off as a soldier, and how he fell for a drum-sergeant's wife, and how he found two ounces of gold in the street, which is what he used to start up his shop in Manzanal . . .'

My master loved Elimas's stories. He bought seven books from him, gave him some money on top of that and a cheese for his journey, and let me take Norés the dog with him as far as Belvís, where he was going to sell the girls of the Countess's family a new story he had with him, then all the rage in Paris, entitled *Paul et Virginie*.

CHAPTER 8

The Hourglass

I was playing bowls with the lad whose father, Antón da Arnega, came to Miranda every year around All Saints to make clogs, and in a week made all the clogs that we should need in the household for a whole year. The father brought the boy with him to prepare the colours and then dye the clogs. His name was Frolentino and he was a bit hunchbacked, and he spent most of the time running after me, wanting me to show him my goldfinches and play bowls with him and tell him stories. Well, as I was saying, we were playing bowls when in through our gate came Don Felices, the cantor in the cathedral of Santiago, a man learned in many mysterious arts, and so far as the better side of him went, a most courtly gentleman and a devotee of Portomarín brandy. He came up on his mule of the Meira breed with its proud, steady stride, his purpose being to ask Merlin to repair an hourglass which he had brought wrapped up in a black velvet bag tied with a red tape. I can see him as if he were still before me now, with his bright expressive eyes, his red nose with its great ridge, his mouth with elegantly formed lips which seemed to be always smiling, and his long arms and huge hands, surprising in a man of no great stature such as he was, hardly taller than the minimum height for army recruits.

'This fellow who's just arrived', said Merlin to me while Don Felices was putting his mule in the stable, preferring not to leave me to do this because the animal was a bit nervous and given to biting, 'is vastly learned, and when it comes to cartomancy, you could call him the walking university of Galicia. We've been friends for years, and it amazes me when I recall the things I've seen him do by his divining, both by cards and by using flour. When you use flour it's called alphitomancy, a very secret business, and it's used especially to find treasure-trove, and people who are in South America, and which widows are having affairs, and what violent deaths will be coming up. I can tell you he actually sees them happen.'

Well, as I was saying, there was Don Felices with his hour-glass, which was a very elaborate piece in the Toledan style, with two snakes as handles, the glass of the container pink, four heads of little cherubs as feet, vine-stems with clusters of grapes forming the columns, the whole thing crowned by a tiny mirror no bigger than the nail on your little finger set in a gold piece of His Majesty King Charles III. Don Felices was asking Merlin to repair the mercury on the little mirror, which had come unstuck one day at the Viana do Bolo fair, when he was doing a divination for young Lord Humoso who wanted to find out who a certain girl was in love with.

The repair job was not all that easy, since what was needed was the purest Italian mercury, and once the work was under way and costs were being incurred it was advisable to change the sand in the hourglass too. This couldn't be done in two or three days, so Don Felices stayed with us, always breakfasting on porridge and roast chitterlings, and we became good friends. The special adornment of his person was silver buckles: he had one on the green ribbon of his hat, four to button his shirt, another four on his tabard, two on each of his suspenders (what firm fat calves he had!) and finally one on each shoe. I polished them all every morning with purified salt, a service for which he was very grateful. Don Felices spent most of the time chatting to my master about *De manticae Variationibus*, and about the daemon known in German as 'Hornspiegel', that is in our language 'horned mirror', who was busying himself in Seville at the time stirring up improper desires among the married ladies. They talked too about a cockerel in Soria that had laid a golden egg in the presence of a lawyer, about the signs which would announce the coming of the *dies irae*, about who had assassinated Prim, about how a railway locomotive works. One problem which Don Felices was being consulted about had turned cathedral chapters upside down: whether in canon law players of flutes, clarinets, oboes, and bugles, should be banned from eating peas and beans, which hang heavy on the breath and deaden the sound of the instruments (the Chapter of Tuy had already issued such a ban). In the afternoons Don Felices went up to read the cards with Lady Guinevere, in order to find out what had happened to all the knights of Brittonia, whether Doña Galiana had got married in her house, whether the Cavamún road had materialized, how many children Don Amadís's grandson would have, whether it was raining or not at the time in Havana, and whether the Tsar of Russia had managed to make la Bella Otero pregnant. Don Felices enjoyed himself hugely as he drew these secrets out of the cards, and when he came out with something which astonished Lady Guinevere or my master, he would smile humbly and say as though talking to himself, 'Never in a month of Sundays will you find a bit of news like that in the papers.'

He read the cards for me one night after supper, first by the method they call 'with your cloak unbuttoned', then 'in the tournament', and finally 'with the priest's stole out in front'. I don't mind confessing that he had got me all sized up, and he even divined that I was crazy about Manoeliña de Calros, and told me that if I worked at it, by Candlemas time three years thence we should be going to the font for a christening. He said that since the string of clubs had come out in order from high to low, and the jack of diamonds was on its own, and the four of hearts appeared right way up between two rows of spades, he was sure the child would be a boy, and cited a little verse to prove it. I stared for a long time at those four red hearts, and that bit of writing in which Heraclio and Co. states its address in Vitoria and claims 'Finest quality playing-cards'. Well, time went by, as it does, and since boys will be boys, I went on teaching Manoeliña how to – if you'll pardon the expression – spit cherrystones, and as it got dark in May we went out to chase the weasels away from the birds' nests, and later Ramonciño was born. Often I looked at him as I was cradling him, but

I never could manage to work out what threads might have run from that four of hearts, finest quality playing-cards, to that lively little plump ball. Don Felices certainly knew his stuff!

My master finally fixed the hourglass, and off went Don Felices on his Meiran mule, in a hurry to get to the fair at Cacabelos, where he wanted to change it for a quieter animal with a better appetite. Ramonciño is somewhere in heaven: about Candlemas time when he was just five, one Shrove Tuesday he was carried off by a fever brought on by measles. Manoeliña and I were married by then, and we lived in Pacios, where I was the ferryman who took people across from the Trigás bank to Mourenza.

'Don Felices knows such a lot!' I exclaimed to my master after we had said goodbye to that walking academy of learning.

'He knows about everything that the eye can't see,' replied Don Merlin, elegantly raising to his nose, on the tips of his fingers, a little pinch of snuff.

CHAPTER 9

Repairing the Silver Princess

God's truth, that day I really thought they were bringing a corpse to Miranda to bury it. First there came a flautist all in black, and after him an acolyte with an incense-burner, then a man on horseback completely shrouded in a purple cape with a hood over his head holding a cross aloft. They passed through the outer gate and lined up over against the wall of the big hayloft. The flautist started to play a mighty sad tune, the acolyte dropped some incense into the burner and swung it to and fro, and the mounted man pulled down his hood to reveal a tonsure of the minor orders, he being (as I learned later) the chief altar-server of my lord the Duke of Lancaster. My master told me to open both gates. He too had dressed in purple, and was wearing the half-mitre to which he was entitled by his degree in both parts of the Medical Tripos at Montpellier, together with the yellow neckerchief of the Faculty. Lady Guinevere appeared on the main balcony with her parasol, because the sun can be pretty fierce there on a September afternoon. I was grieved that there had been no notice given, and that the procession caught me in my old clogs, in my patched smock and my breeches rolled up to the knees. Mistress Marcelina and Manoeliña appeared to strew the yard with roses, fennel, and reedmace, and they were very finely dressed. In through the open gates there then rode two men, with swords at their belts, followed by another who was riding with a Zamoran packsaddle, and that despite the fact that he was a gentleman of distinguished appearance and clearly the highest placed of all that company. In front of him, tied to the packsaddle, he had a box of fine shiny wood with gold adornments and an impressive lock on it. They were all dressed in purple. The men with the swords dismounted and lifted the box down, whereupon the gentleman dismounted too. We could see then that he was an elderly man, finely bearded. He took off his double-brimmed hat and embraced Merlin, and then, turning towards the balcony, he bowed very deeply and elegantly to Lady Guinevere. Don Merlin drew a piece of parchment from his left sleeve and handed it to the gentleman, and the latter then ordered that the box should be placed at my master's feet. Everybody then remounted, the man with the tonsure hoisted the altar-boy up behind him, and with parting salutes to Lady Guinevere, who was still on the balcony with her parasol, and to Don Merlin, they all set off towards Quintás at a gallop. The flautist went over to kiss my master's hand, and I then realized that he was to stay. He was a fat, phlegmatic fellow with red hair, and a thick red moustache heavily waxed. What most struck one about his appearance was the outsize sword he wore hanging from his belt by two straps, across his bottom, so that when you looked at him from the front you saw half a yard of weapon sticking out to one side, with finely-wrought metalwork on the hilt, and on the other side a couple of yards of red scabbard.

'Now, Felipe, you help Master Flute to get the box into our best room. You, Master Flute, can lay your sword in the lance-rack, right beside my lance, which will be honoured by such company; that is, if you want to be able to get through the doors in this house.'

I thought this was worth a laugh, but my master was serious. Master Flute really was a tedious chap. First he put his instrument away in a blue baize bag, having taken it to pieces and dried out all the bits by blowing on them. Next he unhooked his vast imposing sword, and I showed him where to hang it in the rack beside Don Merlin's lance and the shotgun called 'Napoli', the French travelling pistols and the long Moorish gun. Next he took out a herb-scented handkerchief from his breeches pocket amd wiped the sweat off his face, adjusted the points of his moustache, shook the dust off his cap and straightened the white cock's feather he wore in it. Only when all that was done was he able to attend to the order about carrying the box, with me following him and thinking he was as dumb as he was stupid. I could see that Merlin was not very happy with such slow progress, and he stayed close to the box, tapping the floor with his foot and fanning himself with his medical half-mitre. The box didn't weigh more than twenty-two Galician pounds, which would be about twenty-three and a half pounds according to the Medina del Campo measures, this being the standard they now use in the kingdom of León. We put the box on the table and Don Merlin lit the oil-lamp, the one I had always liked so much because on each of its four glass panels it had, worked in coloured brass, scenes of Don Quixote's deeds: the windmills, the convicts from the galleys, the wineskins, and the lion which was being taken to the King. I never tired of looking at these when the lamp was lit.

'Now,' said my master to me in a solemn tone, 'go and shut the outer gate with three turns of the key, shoot the bolt, tell Xosé to turn the dogs loose in the yard, and take Master Flute to the kitchen so that you can both have your supper, since it's already nine o'clock; then you can show him to his bed in the new attic, and tomorrow will be another day.'

Master Flute followed me without a word. In the kitchen he saluted the women with a slight bow when they greeted him, and Marcelina placed before him, on the table by the bench, a dish of bacon rashers rolled in wheat flour and a jar of San Fiz wine. As for talking, Master Flute didn't, but he had evidently missed a meal or two earlier, and he had a second helping of bacon and then a slice off a joint, and then took half a Galician pig's ear which was in the serving-dish and got his jaws round that, chewing away at great speed as a good Englishman should. He took a final draught from the jar of wine, drank it down just like my master, loosened his belt, threw himself back on the bench, and giving me a great slap on the back which made me spit out half an apple I was nibbling, said in a little high voice which made everyone laugh, 'Thanks be, for supper served at last and hospitality offered!' Then he called out 'Cock-a-doodle-doo!' to the three capons which were fattening in their coops, and fell to laughing himself until he cried.

'I didn't speak to you before,' he continued – and now his voice sounded more natural and of a piece with his big moustache – 'because my mouth was dry, or because I had forgotten your language, or because you didn't use a sufficiently formal mode of address to me, or to give you cause for a little gossip, or to have a bit of fun. The fact is that I've had a long, sad journey, lasting many days, doing nothing but offering condolences along the roads, so much so that I don't know if this flute of mine can remember what a dance tune is, and all because of this misfortune that happened to us at Marduffe, some thirty leagues from where the Court of England resides. I'm still not in a mood to tell you about it, but tomorrow, if God wills – and my God is the same as yours – tomorrow, I'll put you in the picture.'

He said all this in a natural, respectful tone, while he was rising from table, and then I took him to his bed in the new attic and showed him where he could find the usual offices. At the door of the kitchen he had turned to smile at Mistress Marcelina and to exclaim, 'I always adored bacon rolled in flour!'

In the morning when I went down to start work Master Flute was still snoring away rhythmically. I soon realized that my master had not been to bed at all, but had sat up all night reading Raymond Llull and Cornelius Agrippa, and at that moment he had Gabir the Arab's work on his lectern, open at the section in which he writes of the weight of the parts of the body in comparison with other materials, all according to the tables of Master Dioscorides. These were all names and books which I loved to bring up in conversation, and they gave me a reputation for erudition. Merlin besides reading had had the furnace alight, for there were still some embers lying in front of it.

'Don't stop to sweep that up now. Come and sit down,' my master said, 'and pay attention, because I'm stuck with a really tricky case, and I want to do my full duty by that old nobleman who brought the box with so much ceremony. Inside that box there lies – in forty pieces, the largest no bigger than a thimble – a highborn lady of the Realm of England, who takes her title from Marduffe Palace. Her name is Lady Lacrima or, in English, Lady Teardrop. I have to admit that getting these princesses properly welded is not easy, and I don't know where to start sticking the parts together, whether from the head end or the foot end, so to speak. This lovely child is made of silver and instead of having bones inside she was encased in glass to hold her together. What happened was that Lord Marduffe found her in a clearing and fell in love with the elegant doll-like creature. Everyone thought she must function by clockwork, so they sent for the chief Swiss watchmaker to check over the mechanism, but Don Omega (that was his name) went to Marduffe and reported that she had no works inside her, no hairspring or second-hand, and that she wasn't any kind of mechanical doll, but had been born a human child. Lord Sweet, who fell very easily in love, was shattered by this, and at once assumed that she was some kind of enchanted princess, in whom he should awaken love and then marry. On the advice of Don Omega they sent for a doctor called Master Hairy from St Andrews in Scotland, whose medical school is so renowned: students there learn to draw up their prescriptions in Latin following Donatus, and learn anatomy according to Vesalius, and concoct purgatives according to Paracelsus, while as for blood-letting and leeches, they follow the school of Salerno, which has prescriptions *ad majores* and also *secundum libidinem*. Master Hairy placed the doll very carefully in warm water, put three drops of rue in her mouth, and by means of a cooling coil fed her with a marmalade electuary, ordering that they should dry her off thoroughly and place her in a bed with two hot-water bottles; they should allow one night to pass, and in the morning a maid should dress her in white silk, and they would soon see around the palace – given that Lord Sweet was so full of both imagination and love – a new princess. The reason why the girl was in that silvery state seemed to be (Master Hairy could find no other explanation among authorities to resolve his doubts) that when her mother was about to give birth to her, somebody in a fury had come and killed the mother with a silver sword or knife at that very instant, the fury passing from the metal into the baby's blood, her body being completely changed thereby. Perhaps the madman had been a husband who awoke to find himself cuckolded, or a rejected lover, and we already know from our history books that in the latter case love does not find that a woman's pregnancy constitutes any sort of barrier. If this is not believed, take the case of Augustus Caesar, who married Lady Livia when she was five months pregnant by another. What manner of thing is love, about which no-one can say when it is born or when it dies?'

Merlin closed the book of Don Gabir. A great big book it was, with clasps in the shape of twining serpents that locked. He took some snuff, blew his nose twice, and was about to go on with the story when Master Flute, now well rested and with his instrument in his hand, asked permission to come in.

'I was just recounting to my page here', said Merlin, 'how Lady Sweet, the same as now lies in pieces in that box, was restored to life in Marduffe Palace.'

'Everything was done', said Master Flute, 'just as Master Hairy had advised. In the morning the senior chambermaid went up with white silk clothing and dressed the doll; her colour changed from silver to that of flesh, she opened her eyes and began to speak very graciously, and since she was hungry she asked for cottage cheese and soft-boiled eggs to be brought. When the news got about lots of people came from the Court at Windsor, since Marduffe is only thirty leagues from there, that is the princes and more than half of the peers and their lordships. In the evening Lady Teardrop made her entry into the Hall of Mirrors on Lord Sweet's arm, myself walking in front trilling a triumphal march on my flute, and all said they never beheld anything lovelier than that sweet child. The Court people were lost for words, but the Duke of Lancaster made bold to ask what her family origins were, to which she answered, in that calm and contented voice which made it seem that she was stroking your ears with a feather, that all she knew about her origins was that they lay way back among Gothic royalty and that she was some kind of niece of Galvans the Landless, and that she had been born in Paris about St Luke's day; though she did vaguely recall having spent a summer in Rome, in a garden with a fountain and two lemon-trees. It was this memory, my lord Merlin, which was the cause of this misfortune, the veil which when drawn back revealed the sin.'

Master Flute wept a few tears, and Don Merlin told him to drink a little mulled wine in order to console himself.

'As for consolation, well yes I do feel consoled, especially as I've made my confession in Santiago with the Canon for the English Language. As I was saying, the whole Court marvelled at this enchanting being, all the peers wanted to dance with her, and the women touched her hair and wished to know what perfume she used, so wonderfully did she smell of fresh-cut roses. Lord Sweet donned a scarlet cloak and announced that he was going to marry Lady Teardrop of Gothia, of Landless, of Paris, of Rome. Everyone congratulated the couple, and the Duke of Wales offered Windsor Castle for their wedding, so that the bride could be presented to the King; but Lord Sweet rejected this, on the grounds that his Gracious Majesty was blind and so in order to assure himself that Lady Teardrop was as perfectly formed and as rich in attributes as everyone said he would have to proceed by touch. I should say she was ... alas!'

Master Flute consoled himself again with two cups of mulled wine I served him. The wine came from the seminary of St John at Ribadavia, in payment of rent due to my master. He tuned the flute and played a sweet little air.

'I composed this dance on paper for the ball which followed my lord's wedding. It's called "The Swan's Pavane" and all England dances it now. The widow of my lord Bishop of Liverpool, the one who puts the saints' calendar into verse each year, wrote a very worthy set of words for it. Well, my lord and

lady married and settled happily at Marduffe, receiving so many
visits from the nobility that the house was as crowded as a
theatre, until one night there arrived a procurator from Calais
in France, by name Monsieur Vermeil.'

'He must be getting on now' – interrupted my master –
'because it must be sixty years since I met him at Rouen in
Normandy, and even then he was white-haired. He was there
on account of an important lawsuit concerning a mermaid, he
being counsel for this dangerous seductress, and I recall that he
was wearing a coarse brown topcoat which seemed to have
suffered some storm damage. He's an expert in both civil and
canon law, certainly, and in some very shady kinds of business
too.'

'Well, he's still wearing that same brown topcoat, though he
has improved it a bit with astrakhan lapels. As for his age, he
doesn't seem to be as old as you think. He had come to Marduffe
as executor of the will of a man who said he was Lady
Teardrop's godfather, this godfather leaving to her the garden
in Rome in which she had been brought up, with running water
twelve days every month, a pew in St Lawrence's Church outside
the city walls, and also a small parrot which cried out all the
time "*Je suis le beau perroquet*". This bird had been deposited
in the house of a member of the Holy Inquisition on suspicion
of heresy and had already cost the Inquisitor four English
pounds for its maintenance. Lord Sweet read over this part of
the will, checked the details of costs, and went off with my lady
and the procurator to Rome, since my lady had a notion to pick
that May – that is, May of last year – a rose in the garden where
she had played as a child. Now Lord Sweet was a Protestant,
but Lady Teardrop had been properly baptized, as she remembered and as the godfather's will confirmed, in the Holy Catholic
Church. When they went into the garden they found that it was
all much neglected, with the pipes of the fountain blocked up,
the strawberry plants eaten up by snails, the climbing vine
without its trellis and fallen on the ground. Only one rosebush
bore roses, just two, one white and one red, and they were over

the roof of the conservatory. Lady Teardrop wanted to climb up to pick them, and m'learned friend Vermeil held the stepladder for her. She cut the roses and was coming down, holding the two flowers in her mouth so as to be able to grasp the ladder with both hands, when there appeared from inside the conservatory – he must have been hiding there for a couple of hours – a tall man dressed in Florentine style, with his face masked. In a mournful voice he said to my lady, who was overcome with astonishment at the top of the ladder, "I knew full well, my beloved, that you would come back! Remember that we are husband and wife and how much we were in love!"

'Lord Sweet on hearing this drew his sword, but the stranger was quicker, and striking over Monsieur Vermeil's head with his long Milanese blade, he pierced Lord Sweet to the heart. Lady Teardrop gave a great cry and fell senseless to the ground, where she shattered into those pieces of silver and glass that are now there in that handsome box. The unknown assailant fled; as he went you could hear the sound of the little bell round his neck, the kind the lepers wear in Florence, in order to warn passers-by to get out of the way. The Pope's police couldn't find out anything about the affair, beyond the fact that my lady was indeed married, in a canonical and consummated union, to Don Giovanni de Treviso d'Aragona, one-time commander of the papal fleet, of whom nothing had been heard since he set out from home one autumn day in order to fulfil a vow made to Our Lady of Loretto. They put Lord Sweet in a barrel of spiced syrup, and Lady Teardrop into that box, and Monsieur Vermeil took ship from Genoa with the two bodies, taking seven weeks to reach Dover because of being becalmed off Lisbon for a time. And now, with the Duke of Lancaster guaranteeing to meet all expenses, the Court of England places these remains in Don Merlin's hands. I say nothing much about myself and my heart which still yearns for her who danced and sang so sweetly to the sound of my merry flute, but I do speak for all who witnessed the dawning of that rose of the day, that mirror of all that is lovely in this world.'

Master Flute was sobbing now, and I was too, so grieved that I went over to him and put my hand on his shoulder, as one would to a good friend. He put his flute to his lips and played a mournful serenade. Tears as big as cherries ran down his fat cheeks and rested like raindrops on his red moustache.

Merlin shut himself up in his furnace-room, saying nothing about how the repairs were going. A whole week went by before he told me to call Master Flute. With that special solemnity and openness which he had, my master explained that it was not easy to solder the Princess together again: 'The only parts I was able to fix are the five fingers on the left hand and her right ear. We could spend a hundred years at it and not finish putting her together. In that garden in Rome at least the tip of her nose must have got lost, and a wisdom tooth. You go home now and report this to his lordship the Duke of Lancaster and Master Hairy. There's something else that concerns me in addition to that, a matter of conscience: I received a letter from Don Giovanni de Treviso, and it is true that he is a leper and now close to death. He asks me to ensure that the lady who was his lawful married wife is buried in consecrated ground. I undertake to attend to that. Most of all I'm sorry for you, my friend, because you'll never play "The Swan's Pavene" again for that unhappy creature.'

Master Flute spent two days weeping, and then departed along the Belvís road. I accompanied him as far as Golpilleira. There was a funeral service in Quintás, at which the secularized monk from As Goás preached very reasonably, emphasizing the vanities of this world and the fact that woman's proper place is in the home. He added a lot about the Moucín pastures being the property of the Abbey of Meira, and said that people who had a notion to buy them (now that they were freed from mortmain) should beware, for there was a smell of gunpowder around some persons' heads. That Riojan priest was certainly some preacher!

CHAPTER 10

The Moor's Mirror

The Moor I'm talking about was as Moorish as they come, the very summit of Moorishness. He wore a red fez and silver rings in his nose and ears, and a serious expression. He was short in stature and had twisted legs, more or less concealed inside his baggy breeches. When he was haggling in merchant fashion you'd find him obstinate and mean, but in conversation he was open enough and inclined to take his time, though he preferred to talk about most things in a confidential tone, as though he were conveying the weightiness of some secret. Since his name was Alsir, which is to be interpreted in our language as 'the secret', you can see that this was in character. He dealt in navigational compasses, instruction manuals about the geometry of plumblines, all kinds of plant essences, and especially story-books of which he always carried a stock, the best-known among these being *Bertoldo, Bertoldino and Cacaseno*, *Guinevere of Brabant*, *The Love-affairs of Galiana la Bella*, and *The Tale of the Devil's Fart*, this last the work of M'sieur Guy Tabarie. On the present occasion, however, he was not coming to Miranda as a merchant, with his customary safeconduct issued by the Sublime Porte, but to seek elucidation of certain scenes which appeared on Saturdays in a mirror that he had, and also to inquire into the case of a desert prince who tried to poison another by getting him to sniff a peach. The attempt at poisoning did not succeed, but ever after Sheikh Rufas remained in a weakened state, and dreamed every night that his eyes were being gouged out with the point of a sword, so that he awoke screaming. Since he spent his days in a state of fear, he became a cruel tyrant and ordered that anyone who glanced at him in a covert way should be topped. They even sent for the English

physician who attended the Khedive of Egypt, who examined
the Sheikh all over, tapped his forehead with little silver hammers and listened to the echo, bled him, and prescribed lard
poultices for his temples, body massages with nutmeg oil,
purgatives of diluted cumin, and cold baths for his private parts,
these if possible in Parkin's Tea, which is the brand favoured by
maiden ladies in England as they prepare to attend Protestant
services in the right frame of mind. Dr Gallows, however, did
not manage to exorcize the fearful dreams, and Sheikh Rufas is
on the verge of madness. It's important to restore him to health
because he is the sole Arab ruler who knows how to pilot the
magic carpet, and the right time to castrate the war-camels; by
tradition, the Sheikh should, at his death, pass these secrets of
science to his youngest son, and if his madness becomes total
these aeronautical and castratory secrets will surely be altogether
lost.

I found out about all this only bit by bit, since as I said Sidi
Alsir liked to wrap his stories up in mysteries, even though to
do so cost him a lot of trouble, since by nature he was really a
rather plain parish-pump kind of chap, except when it came to
money. The mirror in question was of Italian manufacture,
about the size of a half-crown, with a silver frame and a hook
on it in the shape of a dog. It had plainly hung at the end of the
pendulum of a clock, as though the clockmaker who made it
had wanted to have a minute-mirror so that he could study the
languid passing of time. (Well, that's my guess.) Alsir had
bought the mirror at the Tilsit fair from a Khazar Jew who had
a stall there for the sale of peppermints, drinks to encourage
sweet dreams, and good-luck spurs. I learned about this fair
from Sidi Alsir and Elimas the Arab magician. It's twice as big
as the Lyons fair and four times as big as the Monterroso one.
It takes place in a huge field full of stalls and there is an
organization of nine nations, each of which has the right to use
its own system of weights and its own interpreter. The dealers
from other nations have to depend on the weights and legal
services of the Margrave of Brandenburg, who is also present as

a stall-holder at the fair, where he retains the sole right to sell shoes for mules and horses (the rights to donkey-shoeing belong to the sacristans of the Teutonic Knights). A famous fair, I repeat, where you can buy and sell everything, even things that can't be seen. There Alsir bought his mirror, and at Elsinore in Denmark he sold it to a young Countess who lives in the castle there, by name Lady Ophelia. Since it was raining at the time, they offered Alsir lodging in the castle, which has a huge ring of walls set right against the sounding sea, and a garden in the middle protected against the wild winds, under a vaulted roof like you see in churches.

'I was sleeping', Alsir explained to my master Merlin, 'without a care in the world, like a baby, as they say, because I was really tired after all the merchanting in Tilsit, and I had even felt cheerful as I fell asleep, vaguely thinking of fun-and-games with Lady Ophelia, who is all you could wish for in the way of fifteen-year-old Countesses, with their oh-so-white necks … Anyway, I was awoken by loud shouts, being called to go down at once to her ladyship the Countess by her head housekeeper who, although only half-dressed and with her curling-irons still there on the four hairs she had left, was accompanied by a little page-boy who was carrying the hem of her nightdress like a train. Elsinore was always strong on etiquette. They took me to the Countess's room: she was in a fit of sobbing and sighing, laughing and screaming, and Prince Hamlet's physician was trying to get her to calm down by drinking an infusion of lime and aniseed. Everyone was suddenly at me, accusing me of having sold a magic mirror to the young lady: when she had looked into it as she combed her hair on preparing for bed, there had appeared in the mirror four kinds of ghosts, a daemon hanging from a pear-tree, a horse which leaped from the battlements into the sea, and she herself, drowned, floating downstream, with a kingfisher nestling between the sweet apples of her breasts. I had known nothing of the mirror's magical powers, and said as much; they believed me, and I paid back the purchase price, whereupon they instructed me to present myself next morning for an audience with the Crown Prince of Denmark, this Hamlet I was talking about. After that I didn't get a wink of sleep, and I spent most of the night looking in the mirror. What I saw there, in a cloud in front of my face, as it were, was a mass of people dressed in red, the white horse which leaped into the sea, and Lady Ophelia drowned. A bramble branch over the water had caught on her blue dress and caused her lovely body to swing with the current, and now it was her head that the water lapped against on the surface. Her wide, gentle green eyes were open. I was still looking at this when the clock in the tower of the keep struck twelve and the image in the mirror was effaced. All I could see, very bright, was my black face lit by the candle. I learned later that the scenes appeared in the mirror only on Saturdays, from dusk to midnight. I saw many things, some of which have already come to pass.'

Sidi Alsir fell silent, as if some painful shadow had settled over his mind. My master, wiping his spectacles on the silk lining of his jacket, said very solemnly, 'This mirror of yours, Alsir, is as familiar to me as my own house, since I had a hand in its manufacture. It was commissioned by the Signoria of Venice – which is the most secretive kind of government of any nation on earth – its purpose being to foretell the future. Well, when mixing the metals I rather overdid one of the ingredients, and this damnable mirror, as I learned later, began to weave things of its own invention in among the future truths. The upstart gadget even invented people, leading the lords of Venice to chase about madly seeking out an assassin who existed only in the mirror's imagination, and investigating deaths, shipments of spices and Turkish vessels, buried treasures and cups full of resolutive liquids, all of which the mirror had invented. Now, my friend, I propose to buy it from you for whatever you paid for it in Tilsit, plus some interest, and then I'll break it into a thousand pieces without waiting for tomorrow, which is a Saturday, when I might see in it Lady Ophelia drowned and carried along by that Danish river which is on its way to the sea.

Maybe that image of Ophelia is one of the few true ones which my mirror has provided for some time past.'

Merlin rose, went over to the drawer in the big table, took out his little bag of gold, and counted out coins worth an ounce and a half, good legal tender, which he dropped one by one into Alsir's hands clasped like a bowl. Alsir counted them all again before slipping them into his pocket.

'There, just as your lordship orders, I obey. You know, Don Hamlet, when I went into that audience with him, already had some inkling of what that mirror was up to. The Prince was sitting as he usually did on the stone armchair with the snake worked on it, and he was stroking a skull. He ordered me to sit at his feet, and told me courteously, in that thoughtful, lordly way he has, that the mirror could not be a true foreteller of the future, and that what it mirrored had no legal authority. "I do not wish to have it here in Denmark," he said to me, "since I have quite enough to do on each day of the present without causing myself worry about the future. No-one is holding a thread to lead us through this airy dream that we call life. So far as Lady Ophelia is concerned, don't you think that the mirror could be comparing her with a rosebush on a riverbank, a bush from which, some blessed summer's day, a rose must inevitably fall into the water, to be borne gently away? Take your mirror out of my kingdom, Alsir, and if it should prove one day that what you saw on its mercury was true, it would be best for you to smash it against a rock on your road." That is what Prince Hamlet said. He rose from his chair, wrapped the tail of his black cloak around his left arm, and placed the skull on the windowsill. In a friendly but sad tone, he bade me farewell.'

Merlin smashed the mirror in his big mortar, stirred salt and a head of Zamoran garlic in among the thousand fragments, and as he ordered I put it all to heat up in his furnace. As treatment for Sheikh Rufas, my master prepared a special medicine and some purgative pills, and begged Alsir particularly to send him news about the health of the castrator-prince. The Moor presented me with a copy of *The Tale of the Devil's Fart*, as a reward for looking after his donkey so well, and because I had managed to cure the animal of a wart she had on her nose.

'I didn't care to tell Sidi Alsir', my master said, as soon as the Moor had gone, 'that Lady Ophelia did indeed die. She was tripping merrily along the riverbank picking daisies, fell into the water, and drowned. I tell you, young Felipe, there's no prince in all this wide world who has greater cause to feel sad than my lord Hamlet, Prince of Denmark.'

CHAPTER 11

The Golden Beam

The dwarf from the castle came up one morning to speak to my master in great secrecy. I could tell that he was in a wary frame of mind and had news of some importance to convey, since he didn't waste time with his usual affected ways, such as keeping me at the outer gate while I bowed properly to him, tightened his stirrup straps, and brushed the dust off his shoulders with my cap. He threw his umbrella to me, leaped off his mare, and with the most brazen air went straight in to speak to Don Merlin without pausing to knock at the door of the furnace-room. The fat little chap thought himself well up in the world, what with knowing French and putting up his hair with different-coloured ribbons. I tied the mare up in the shade and went about fitting a new strip of leather to the smaller grind-stone we use for sharpening knives, and I was just testing my Taramundi penknife for sharpness when Don Merlin called for me and I went along at once. My master was walking up and down looking very grave, and the dwarf, who was sitting on the chest which did duty as a bench, was so short that he couldn't touch the floor even with the tips of his shoes.

'Felipe, my lad,' said Don Merlin to me, 'this very day at nightfall you've got to go off on a journey, without telling a soul where you're going nor why. Dress up in your best clothes, hang this little silver bell round your neck, take the housekeeper's mule and put our big apple-picking basket on it, being sure it's good and clean, with a clean blanket on the bottom to serve as bedding. Go along the Pacios road as far as the pool. When you get there, put the basket on the grass among the Os Cabos rocks, with its lid raised; you go and sit with your back to the basket, and don't stir or make any sound until you hear a long whistle. Then you go over to the basket, without looking at it, let the lid down, put the peg through the wicker ring to close it, and then put the basket on the mule. It may weigh a bit heavy, but I'll telepathize some extra strength to you. Then come back at a steady canter to Miranda.'

'What if that other lot should appear on the road?' asked the dwarf, who I could see was in a pretty nervous state.

Merlin was reassuring: 'Take a few boxes of Portuguese matches with you, and if you think you can see little dogs jumping about on the roads like mice, get the mule moving faster and keep striking the matches. You can call out too, if you like, that you can see their curly tails.'

I just loved these errands! I was so excited I could hardly eat my lunch, and it was no more than five o'clock when I had the mule out in the yard, complete with basket and blanket, and I was already dressed in my coat and wearing my newly-soled clogs. To pass the time I made a new boxwood peg for the basket, nicely rounded at both ends. The castle dwarf, who was strutting about in the yard from the outer gate to the house and back again, very conceited with his straw hat and his rapier, took his watch from his pocket, put it to his ear, and told me the time. He took a look at the new peg, and told me to try closing the basket with my eyes shut, seeming content with the result to the extent that he clapped me on the back and said I was really a man now. The moment the sun set over beyond Meira, my master appeared on the balcony and told me to mount and set off, sticking to my orders to the letter; he added that his thoughts would be with me at every moment. I had a little laugh as I rode out, because the dwarf had to roll a stone over and stand on it to reach the bolt and open the gate for me. I felt tempted to demand that he should take off his straw hat to me, just as I took off my cap to him. I turned off into the old road, practising lighting matches without letting go of the bridle or disturbing the animal's gait, then I made her trot so that the bell I had round my neck jingled a bit, for all the world as if some crazy altar-boy were performing some duty among the

garden plots as night came down. Almost before I realized it I
reached Os Cabos, and with mist coming up over the pool the
night got very dark. I followed my orders, varying them only
because the mule was rebellious and would not settle, but I
tethered her to one of the rocks and gave her an apple, after
which she seemed more at ease. There can be few places in the
world more silent than the big Esmelle pool when it isn't frog-
mating time. When the castle dogs began to bark I could hear
the whole chorus start up, because next it was the Pacios dogs,
then the Seixedo dogs, then the Piñeiro ones further off, and
ours, and finally the Belvís huntsman's bitch. It seemed to me as
I listened to those familiar barks that I had company with me,
but just then my ear caught the whistle, coming from so close
that I could feel the blast of air on the back of my neck. I waited
a few seconds, turned towards the basket, and without even
trying to look I put the lid down and secured it with the peg,
and then carried it without the slightest effort over to the mule.
Evidently Don Merlin's telepathized help had come in handy. I
mounted and rode off at a trot across the meadow, and since
Marcelina's mule finds that pace just right, she went off easily
and gracefully along the Miranda road. The creatures that the
dwarf had mentioned, 'the other lot', did not come out to play,
but just in case I lit a couple of matches, tinkled my bell a bit,
called out that I could see curly tails, and reached Miranda
feeling just a trifle nervous because I could hear moving and
breathing noises from inside the basket, and a sort of conversation like hens cackling.

The gate stood open, and Xosé do Cairo, also dressed in new
clothes, was holding aloft the lantern on a stick which Don
Merlin and Lady Guinevere carry in the St Bartholomew procession at Seixo. The door of the furnace-room was wide open too,
all the lamps were lit inside, and there stood the dwarf with his
straw hat in his hand, and my master with his double-thickness
cloak and his academic cap with the tassel. I got the basket
down off the mule and my master raised the lid, whereupon
instantly there leaped out six tiny fellows all dressed up in green

and red, with huge hats, and they all – with one exception – knelt down and took off their hats in front of Merlin. The one who remained standing made a low bow, with one foot behind him, and bade everyone good-evening in that cackling voice I had heard along the road.

'It has been many years, my lord Prince,' said my master very respectfully to the tiny person, 'since we met in Truro, when you were studying at the school there, and were living in the capacious sleeve of my cousin the subcantor, may he rest in peace.'

The one addressed as Prince made another bow, taking half a step back, and followed Don Merlin into the room, the other five mini-men and the castle dwarf going after. I was amazed to find what a company I had transported: so amazed that I forgot to put the mule into her stable, and to blow out the lantern which Xosé do Cairo, who knew I never minded the joke, stuck right under my nose.

I couldn't bear to leave the yard or take myself off to bed until I knew what the outcome of the discussion might be, so I sat myself at the foot of the fig-tree and struck the Portuguese matches I had left. I was still playing with them when the castle dwarf came out to tell me to bring a few pastries and some mulled wine. On the pretext of serving these I was able to intrude myself into the room, where I found the miniscule host sitting on the chest, my lord the Princekin in my master's armchair, and Don Merlin on the padded stool reading his Latin books, while the dwarf stood next to the lectern holding the candlestick and turning the pages for Merlin, though for this he had to stand on a measure of corn to reach the required height. My master read aloud in a booming voice, sounding like a priest reading the Epistle, and the little Prince paid close attention, being expert in that science, while the other members of the group bit noisily into the pastries after dipping them in the wine.

'That is what Don Cornelius Agrippa lays down,' said Merlin, concluding his reading and taking off his tortoiseshell spectacles.

'I belong to a different school of thought, but in this most arcane matter I agree with him to the letter. The golden beam, on which the second arch of the earth rests, corresponds to the last four bones of the coccyx in man, and among the stars it corresponds to what the Arabs call the Tahali, which we Christians call the Three Marys. The second arch of the earth has one end based in Armagh in Ireland, where St Patrick's Well is, and the other end is in Rome, under the basilica of St John Lateran; and the central voussoir is situated right over the imperial city of Aix-la-Chapelle. So that thick vein of gold which you encountered when you were digging to extend your bowling-green is part of the golden beam, and if you were to start turning it into coin in your mints, it's sure that in two or three years half France would collapse, and there would hardly be a furrow left to show where Flanders had been. Furthermore, in my opinion the doubloons you might strike would not be enough to pay the ransom you have in mind for Doña Carolina's daughter.'

'That daughter of Doña Carolina,' cackled the Prince, 'is our queen and our sovereign, and the Little People feel they have been orphaned ever since she went to learn embroidery and the art of making almond cakes with the Dauphine of Thule, while I, her Don Paris, her future husband, grow old in bachelorhood. We know, from messages that came via London, via Scotland Yard to be precise, that she is living in a silver cage, disguised as a fantail pigeon, a state to which she is well suited, being as petite and elegantly made as she is. But the Dauphine of Thule, who is an unreliable old party, laughs when she complains about her loneliness, and says she won't let her return to us unless we come up with compensation in the form of eleven crops of Palermo almonds and a thousand yards of Murcian silk, these being the quantities our dear lady Queen wasted when she was learning to cook and to sew. You can see why we were thinking of turning that secret vein of gold into coin, and this is why we came to Miranda to consult you, since we need to know about the royal cypher of Thule and what arms to put on the reverse of the coins.'

Tears began to well up in Prince Paris's eyes, and on seeing this his men began to weep copiously, though this did not prevent them continuing to nibble the pastries, which had come from the St Clare Convent, and had been dipped in syrup by my mistress, Lady Guinevere.

'The royal cypher of Thule,' explained Merlin, 'is a crow in a little boat, and the arms are the fleurs-de-lis of France, which passed to the family through an aunt once removed, who had a child on the side by a Frenchman who was shipwrecked on the coast of Thule. He was something of a musician and was in charge of all the ironing and starching for the Court at Versailles. Lady Fog, the aunt once removed, took him aboard, so to speak, and the people of Thule called him Prince Scarefly, he being the grandfather of the Dauphine currently in office, Miss Spindle by name. Thulean money is not of gold but of amber, gold there being as common as iron is here, so far as its worth is concerned. If you don't believe me, ask the dwarf of Belvís here present, because he went there as cupbearer when they took Doña Carolina's daughter to Thule.'

The dwarf blushed, all his arrogance now gone, and hid behind my master, while the little men who were sitting on the chest, on hearing that detail, stood up and put their hands on the swords that swung from their belts; but Prince Paris calmed them with great authority, declaring, 'The dwarf is completely blameless in this matter, since he undertook that journey for money, just as he served us as a messenger for money just now. I can tell you that as a servant of Doña Carolina he was quick and courteous, and I heard that two leagues from London, while travelling in the worst of the heat of a torrid summer in that country, he paid out of his own pocket for a tutti-frutti ice-cream for her ladyship.'

With these words he managed to calm his army down. Don Paris and all his men went off weeping when, at dawn, we returned them to the apple-basket with the same formalities with which we had received them: Xosé with the lantern on the pole, my master with his double cloak, and the dwarf with his straw hat in his hand. I took them off to Os Cabos; the new day was dawning over the world when I let them out among the rocks, and down through a crack in the biggest rock they departed from this land into the realms below. I grieved for Prince Paris, so much in love, with his little moustache and bright eyes, and if the captive lady really was the size of a dove, as they said, they certainly would have made a happy pair. When I got back to Miranda my master was waiting for me at the outer gate.

'If those inhabitants of the underworld really do set about turning the golden beam into coin', he said as he helped me to put the mule in her stall, 'I think the crack-up of the world might stretch from Cambrai to Mondoñedo.'

'And what was that tale about "the other lot"?'

'The lands of the underworld, my lad, are as much parcelled up as lands here on earth. These fellows that came to us just now are a Christian people, related to the Chaldees, and their sole object in life, ever since they were consigned to the depths, is to search for the serpent Smarís, whose eggs, each as big as your head, if you'll pardon the comparison, have in them an essence which if filtered through a cock's crest will make the little people grow big if they drink it. That is, these people who seem no bigger than grains of millet in this world will become a race of giants. So they burrowed in the earth and took their mine galleries in so many directions that they eventually ran up against the Corantines, a race which was at that moment celebrating a secret kind of gathering; they are keepers of treasures, who disguise themselves as tiny dogs – like those little dogs in Flemish paintings – by placing curly tails on their caps, in order to hold their festivities. The Chaldees made fun of them, and the two groups fell out, and now, when the Corantines sense that a Chaldee is emerging into this world here above, they come up too, tricking the Chaldees into taking the wrong road or forgetting the message they were carrying, and only by means of bells, lights, and references to their curly appendages, can the tail-bearing beasties be held in check. Well, you'll have learned so much about underworld geography that you could sit an examination in it at Sagres, but off you go to bed now: tomorrow is a new day, and we have a visitor of some importance.'

CHAPTER 12

The Greek Mermaid

I didn't wake up until it was gone twelve, and breakfast was already on the table: I always loved that sweet pumpkin soup that mistress Marcelina made in autumn, so much so that I generally had a second helping. I stayed on an hour in the kitchen telling them the tale of Don Paris and the prisoner of Thule, and I was going to go on with it when I heard my master calling for me. My problem was that Manoeliña was right there beside me, peeling chestnuts, and with that look she kept giving me she seemed to be encouraging me to go on: I must have sounded like one of those male blackbirds trying to attract the female with the grace-notes of his song ... I went off to obey my master's call, however, and found him with Xosé do Cairo putting our big washing-tub, which was half a Valdeorras hogshead that held forty-eight gallons, down right in the middle of the room. The seamstress from Pacios was there too, draping a sort of pleated skirt round the tub, very elegant, with green and red flowers on it. Lady Guinevere came down to see the show and, after Xosé and I had half-filled the tub with water, her ladyship poured a little flask of perfume into it, which smelled of cinnamon. Don Merlin was in a cheerful mood: he smiled broadly, scribbled some numbers on his blackboard, and said to Lady Guinevere, who was smiling too, 'If she hasn't put on more than two pounds, she'll be able to get into the tub without slopping a single spoonful over the side.'

I soon learned – well, there was no other subject of conversation in Miranda that evening – that we were expecting a Greek mermaid, by name Lady Theodora: her lover, a Portuguese viscount, had died, and in her grief she wished to enter a convent which these ladies have deep in the lake of Luiserne. She was coming to us so that my master could prepare to give notice of this in the Pont Mathilde Court at Rouen, which is the judicial body that issues rulings concerning these females. She also wanted Merlin to dye the scales of her tail in suitably deep mourning.

'Be sure you don't dye her in perpetual deep mourning,' observed Lady Guinevere to my master, 'because one fine day she might have second thoughts and go looking for a new lover, right there in Luiserne.'

'I am aware of that possibility', replied Merlin, 'and I know how hard it is for these creatures to give up their whorish habits even when they are duly converted Christians. I knew one once who tried to take poison because her lover had died (he was second soprano in the Pope's chapel choir, in Rome), saying she couldn't live bereft of their musical duo, and of the pasta dish he cooked for her on Sundays. She sent me a message, in writing, asking for a resolvent syrup, but by the time I sent back word to say "No", she had already set up house with the coast-inspector of Honfleur, who built a lobster tank for her. From that time until just recently she had at least four foremen in the business, one after the other, and bedded each of them, if you'll pardon the expression. Can you believe it, she even had a go at me one summer when I went to Calais beach to bathe my feet!'

My master and Lady Guinevere laughed. Her ladyship told Marcelina to put the hake in the sluice by the well, to keep cool. All of us at Miranda, I think, were on tenterhooks about the outcome of this great affair.

The party of travellers arrived at nightfall, all on big mules: the mermaid as a sorrowing widow with long silken veils, two riders who were afterwards revealed to be relatives and heirs of the deceased Portuguese, and a page-boy aged about fourteen, who rode on the crupper of the mermaid's mule and held aloft a huge umbrella in such a way as to turn the rain onto the suffering lady. Xosé do Cairo lifted Lady Theodora down, took her indoors and sat her in Merlin's armchair, while one of the Portuguese, Senhor Almeida, a tall man with thick black moustachios, saluted Lady Guinevere and Don Merlin and begged pardon for their late arrival, caused by the fact that as they came from Braga in three days they had to pause at the Miño river so that Lady Theodora could have a good soak for a couple of hours. Theodora, sitting comfortably in the armchair, removed her mourning veils with the help of the Pacios seamstress, and I have to tell you that if the Lord ever created roses few could compare with this one, and her eyes were two green dewdrops. When she leaned back a little in the chair, you could see the end of her tail, a lovely pink crescent, peeping from under her long skirt. If I say I was overcome, that doesn't really do justice to the state I was in.

'Madam, Lady Theodora,' began my master very formally, 'this house at Miranda is yours while you are in it. We all sympathize with you in your loss of so faithful a love as you enjoyed on the sands of Portugal. This lady you see before you is our mistress Lady Guinevere, Princess of Brittonia, these are my servants, and this is my page Felipe, whom I place at your service for any errand. And this scented tub is your bed. Now I propose to write the announcements you desire. The dye for putting your tail into deep mourning is all ready.'

If only you could have heard that lovely lady's voice! She sang rather than talked. Some birds have a mysterious song, but there's no possible comparison: if only I could listen to her in the mornings rather than to the dove!

'I can see how grieved you all are on account of the treasure I've lost, and it is true there's no lover to compare with a Portuguese! My Lady Guinevere, Madam, I kiss your hands, and I salute Don Merlin, and the whole of this household, and the page you have assigned to me. I am indeed in a great hurry, because you know that on St Luke's day I must be at the Luiserne convent gate with my head shaved.' As she said this she stroked her long golden hair with both hands: it was like a violin bow lingering over four well-tuned strings.

Since there was such urgency, the two Portuguese gentlemen went to sup at Lady Guinevere's table, and her page and I sat in the outer room while my master put the final touches to his dyeing preparations. Lady Theodora said all she wanted for supper was a bit of raw hake, from the upper part of the fish, and for dessert just a spoonful of salt and a small cup of coffee liqueur. Her page, whose name was Theophilos (he was Greek) and I served her this on a silver tray. Every so often she gave me a sweet smile which tugged at my heart. When she had finished supper she suggested that she might be more comfortable in the tub: I didn't know which way to look when she took her long skirt and tight-fitting blouse off and her ladyship displayed herself with all those lovely attributes depicted in story-books. Well . . . I'd never seen a woman naked before, and although I tried to stop them, my eyes kept going towards those white breasts, so beautifully shaped, with their little pink buds and the blue veins that furrowed the snowy whiteness. I suppose Theophilos was used to all this, but for me the display was part merry but part awesome too. I even had to get close to her, following Theophilos, since she had to put her arms round our necks; and she wiggled her long shiny tail a bit as we popped her into the tub to rest. Whenever I recall this incident, I can still feel my body caressed by the gentle warmth that flowed from her. I think it was just as well that as soon as she was in the tub she put an astrakhan cape on which covered up these delightful sights.

My master then came along with the documents he had composed: the announcement for the Pont Mathilde Court, compensation for the nephews of a Genoese apothecary, and a profession of Christian faith; all that was lacking was Lady Theodora's signature, which she added with a series of great flourishes, together with some Latin which Don Merlin dictated to her. 'We mermaids', she said to my master with a smile, 'all have the same handwriting, since we all learned it together at the School of Penmanship at Iturzaeta.'

The moment for the dyeing had now arrived. We put a stool in the tub so that when Lady Theodora sat on it, the liquid should cover only her pink tail. In the midst of these preparations I noticed – my gaze may have been sinful but was genuinely curious too – that the lady had no navel. Don Merlin did a bit of chanting and addressed the water in a language I couldn't understand, then poured a concoction in: sulphate of gold in powder form, four different mixtures of walnut bark, extract of Campeachy wood, and cream of tartar. He stirred away for an hour with a little silver rod, then threw in a handful of salt, and declared the process over.

'Your tail will come out', he said to Lady Theodora, 'a shiny black colour, the one they call "Neapolitan raven" in Italy, and all round the edge of each scale there'll be a bright gold thread. Ever since Don Amadís died, and Lady Oriana went into perpetual mourning, there's not been a more dignified expression of grief seen in the world. You should spend all night in the dye, and you can go off to Luiserne at first light.'

Lady Theodora ordered Theophilos to hand over to my master a purse full of tinkling coins. 'I know full well that I cannot repay all the favours I have received in this house, but there in the purse you have, in the form of florins, all that is left of my former fortune; not earned by any attractions of my body when made available, but inherited from a sister of mine, the mistress of a Roman cardinal, a girl you'll have heard of, because he secured permission for her to live in the river that runs through the city; each year she put together two sackfuls of the various coins dropped by the pilgrims as they crossed the bridge.'

My master thanked her for the gift, Theophilos stretched out on the chest to have a snooze, and Don Merlin and I went off to our beds, not forgetting to bow deep to her ladyship the mermaid. I should tell a lie if I were to say that I got to sleep that night, since my body was wracked by a continual fever of restlessness. It gnawed at me for days on end, and even though I'm an old man now, at times I go into a sort of daydream, turning round suddenly because I seem to hear, within the music of the water as it runs past my boat, that soft singing speech of hers, and then I ask myself – half in verse, part-mad, part in jest – Can you really still want anything of me, Lord Love?

I was ready while it was still dark, in my new cap, and Lady Theodora was up and dressed, but she had donned an open skirt of merino wool which exposed her beautiful tail all the way from waist to crescent tip, now dyed for deep mourning, and just as my master had said, each scale was edged with a bright gold thread which suited her splendidly. Senhor Almeida and His Excellency Novás had already mounted; Xosé do Cairo and my master helped Lady Theodora on to her mule, with a blanket wrapped round her tail, and Theophilos climbed up on to the crupper with the umbrella, since it was still raining. The Portuguese gentlemen uttered the usual Portuguese courtesies, Lady Theodora warbled her thanks and sad farewell, and on the balcony there appeared Lady Guinevere to wave goodbye with an embroidered hankie. Merlin realized, as they departed, that I was feeling pretty downcast, that I had some thread of the mermaid's seductiveness still draped around my neck.

'Easy, easy, young Felipe,' he said, patting me on the back. 'You can't catch trout if you want to keep your breeches dry. Anyway, what could such an other-worldly being want of a well-set-up lad like you except life itself? I wouldn't want to see you appear one day on the Arousa beach eaten up by the fish.'

'Also, you know,' added Xosé do Cairo, who always talked very sound sense, 'also, to judge by the rather chubby tip of her tail, I guess that if she were a normal sort of woman, she'd have fat legs.'

That was all he said. Then he spat in disgust. I burst into tears.

CHAPTER 13

The Trip to Pacios

My master decided to go to Pacios, the reason being that a
friend who was coming to visit him was detained by illness at
the inn there. He was Swiss, a dealer in crystal balls containing
snowstorms of the prettiest kind. What had happened was that
he had come out in a sudden sweat on the road; thinking that a
double rum-punch was just what he needed to set him up, he
ordered one, but here he was a week later still in bed with the
fever still upon him. Merlin asked me if I had ever seen
snowballs of that sort or framed pictures with snowstorms going
on, and I said 'No'. The only sort of snow I had seen was out in
the countryside, except once in the Teatro Ideal do Valenciano
in Lugo, during the San Froilán festivities, when they produced
pretend snow with flour in the scene where the wolves were
howling at Don Cruces' door, when he lay inside dying in a
series of fits halfway through the performance, the point being
that until the final curtain we didn't know that he had been
poisoned by his niece.

'In that case', Don Merlin said, 'I'll make you a present of this
trip to Pacios, and I'll ask M'sieur Simplon to show you the
whole range of his wares.'

On the way, my master riding and I walking three paces in
front as the custom is, he told me that M'sieur Simplon had
been personal watchmaker to the Dukes of Savoy, and that the
two had become friends when Merlin was in Turin to remove
the spell from Duke Philibert the Elder: one of those weaver
daemons had got into his Grace's person, and was at his loom
day and night, with the result that his Grace spent his time both
spitting and shitting bits of cloth which the pesky creature had
woven in the workshop of his belly. They got the daemon out

all right, but his lordship was in a delicate state after the operation, and soon after he suffered a palsy and died. Now his successor the new Duke had not the faintest interest in the craft of watchmaking, and devoted all his time to playing cards. He dismissed M'sieur Simplon, but not before taking off him, at a game called *juleppe au carré*, his final pay-packet and a vineyard and windmill in Alessandria della Palla, which had been a bequest from Duke Philibert. All this despite the fact that M'sieur Simplon had been a very unwilling participant in the game, his distaste for cards being perfectly well known to all at court. An old man now, and penniless, M'sieur Simplon took up the manufacture of snowballs worked with springs, and was on his way to Portugal to sell a dozen to my Lord Bishop of Lamego, who was so crazy about such things that he used to demonstrate one, which he had bought in Rome, to the faithful from his pulpit: it showed the Nativity at Bethlehem, and the people wept when they saw thick snow falling on the Child, lying naked in the straw.

We were chatting about all this when we reached the river. I crossed by the stepping-stones, of which there are seventeen, in a series of jumps, while my master trotted across the ford, our horse Luceiro throwing up the spray with that free-striding gait of his. The whole river-bank there is one vast apple-orchard, and the valley a series of meadows. We were in Pacios well before eleven, going into the yard of O Liaño's inn, which has a climbing vine that extends over the whole balcony of the sun gallery. Mine host emerged to greet Merlin in the friendliest way. When Merlin asked about the sick man's condition, O Liaño replied that it did not look good for, according to the quack doctor of Arnois, the fever had reached his pulses, which were no longer beating in time, and the blood-letting had left him in a faint from which he was slowly recovering with the aid of a thick soup laced with sherry. O Liaño was an ugly man, as fat as they come, with a Kaiser Bill moustache, which he wore only to give an air of gravity, since he was really one of the funniest and jolliest people you could wish to meet. When he had had a few drinks, he did an impression of the inn's Leonese cellarman, and everyone fell about laughing. He took us up to M'sieur Simplon's room. We found the Swiss almost at his last gasp, sweating under nine blankets; you could just see the sharp tip of his nose emerging from the sheets, his bald head being half hidden by a white stocking with blue stripes, which made a funny kind of nightcap. My master went up to the bed, felt for M'sieur Simplon's hand under the bedclothes, and then called out loudly 'Bonjour!' A full minute went by before the patient opened his left eye, fixed his gaze on my master, and in a voice that suggested he was already on his way to the next world, moaned in reply: 'Ah, Merlin, Merlin, I've really had it this time!'

My master, as a qualified physician, began to feel his body, checked his temperature with his serpentine stone, asked him to stick his tongue out, put a drop of vespers water in his right ear, and listened for a while to the rhythm of both pulses. He thought things over for a quarter of an hour, and then, to judge by his expression, came up with the answer to the problem.

'The whole of this complaint', he declared, 'stems from the fact that the humours of his body went above boiling-point, since it was a fever of the memory that he had, and now it's hard to bring the humours back to their proper level. These humours form layers in the body, like – it might be – fat and lean in a rasher of bacon, or oil and water in a lamp. What happens is that if they get out of order or mixed up, they soften your insides. But it's also rather worse than that in the present case, because this M'sieur Simplon was pretty quick to sin against the sixth commandment, and he doesn't have much juice left in his wineskin.'

Don Merlin brought in his medicine bag, and made up a dose of spirits of senna and a purgative wine. He sent O Liaño's nephew off to the apothecary's at Meira to fetch a theriac and pills of sedative honey, hoping that with these remedies and the quinine he was already taking the patient would achieve the necessary relief. 'I'll meet all the costs', said Merlin to O Liaño, 'because this Swiss gentleman is a dear friend of mine.'

The Swiss, with the spirits of senna, and perhaps aided also by my master's soothing, friendly words, recovered a little, stuck his white goatee beard above the bedclothes, and began to talk some French to Don Merlin. Merlin went to the iron-bound chest at the foot of the bed, opened it with the key which was in the lock, and began to take out the crystal snowballs, each wrapped in coloured cloth. What a sight they were! O Liaño called for his wife and daughter and small nephew, and with them there came up the blacksmith's children, then the blacksmith and his wife, who was – on the wrong side of the blanket, as they say – a daughter of the former young lord of Humoso. My job was to take each ball as my master unwrapped it and carry it out into the corridor to display it to the whole gathering, whose members were sitting on the attic stairs to see the show. The first ball had one of the Swiss Papal Guard on sentry-go with his halberd at the ready: he took two steps forward and did a half-turn, whereupon it started to snow, and the guard went into his sentry-box. The second ball showed a shepherdess sitting on a wall with her sheep around her, and since this was a musical ball, it seemed as if she was singing; when the snow started, the girl opened her umbrella and the sheep ran to snuggle up to her. In another ball – I was specially fond of this one – a gentleman with a hat was standing beneath a window paying court to a lady with a pompadour hair-do, and when it started snowing and the gentleman was getting covered, a servant with a broom dashed out of the house and brushed him off. This one had music as well, and my master said it came from *The Merry Widow*; he explained the plot to me, and I passed it on to the public. Another ball showed a gentleman on horseback; when the snow began, the horse, a pretty little bay animal, pawed the snow. The whole art of making the snow fall and fly about was in a balance-wheel, and you wound up the balls just as you do a watch. Another I put on display had a guitarist playing a serenade, and in another there was a hermit who pushed the snow aside with his staff, whereupon red flowers sprang from the soil, on which my master remarked that the hermit was the living image of St Goar Alpinus. We saw too the ball of the wild-boar hunter, the one in which a pilgrim is being chased by a wolf, another with the great 1861 snowfall in Paris, another in which an Italian girl with a parasol takes a walk and when it starts to snow goes indoors and then it clears again, and then another of the great snowfall at the burial of the Emperor of Austria when the archbishop's mitre filled with snow, and last of all, this one with music too, a waltz, a ball which showed a Frenchwoman who when most snow was falling came to the door of her house and lifted her skirt right up to show a very well-turned leg, with a black stocking and scarlet garter. We were just waiting for the clockwork of this one to run down when M'sieur Simplon said, in a voice that was half a snore, as though he were waking up, 'If I should die away from my house, I call you to witness that I wish to be buried with that toy in my hands. If you press the button underneath, it winds it up for seven days.'

My master advised him to turn his mind to other things, for he might still enjoy an hour of laughter when showing it to the Bishop of Lamego. And if it was indeed his time to die, it would be better for him to reckon up his soul's accounts than to be stealing a glance at a bit of French leg.

O Liaño's nephew got back from Meira with the theriac and pills of sedative honey; and when Merlin had dosed the patient, we left him dozing while we went down to eat. After lunch there was as much of an audience present to watch Merlin wipe his mouth and wash his hands as there had been to see the snowballs. We went up to see how the Swiss was going on, and found him awake and bright-eyed, and occupied in combing his beard.

'I do believe, my lord magician,' he said to Merlin, 'that I'm cured.'

'I think so too, and there's no miracle about it, because the theriac has such power that either it carries the sufferer far from the deceits of this world, or cures him on the instant. Let us give thanks to the Lord that we got here in time.'

All this and much else my master said to the Swiss in French, and he gave him, as I learned later, a doubloon to help him on his way. M'sieur Simplon rewarded Merlin with a snowball: my master invited me to choose one, and I preferred the one with the man on horseback going through the wood, since I was greatly taken with the bay horse, and the tune on the little bells which the ball made from the box below it. Since it gets dark quickly in autumn, Merlin resolved that we should get back to Miranda without delay, so that we could get past Pontigo while it was still light, for the wolf would be howling in the deep parts between San Lucas and Santos. He told me to get up behind him and ride side-saddle. We went at such a fast trot that it seemed the evening was stretching out for us. 'We must look like the old Abbot of Meira when he went to sign legal documents at Lugo, for he always took a young lay-brother behind him, just like you, riding side-saddle, so that his shanks couldn't be seen.'

Night had still not fallen when we passed by the priest's house at Seixo, but already in the distance we could see, bright and welcoming, the lights of our house at Miranda.

CHAPTER 14

The Road Was Like An Old Beggar

Roads are like furrows: as furrows produce wheat, so do roads produce people, inns, languages, nations. With a road, you can travel along it, or sit beside it and take your harvest in. This road I'm talking about now is rather like an old beggar, even though each traveller who treads it renews it, and manages to revive some portion of early youth on its broken, dusty surface. From Miranda, I can see a stretch of the French Road, the Pilgrims' Way, the Way of St James, go down to look for the ford across the river. It descends from a hill covered with chestnut-trees, and hurries across a flat piece full of rye patches and young maize plots down there towards the water, where it meets a long procession of trees that love the waterside, willows, Lombardy poplars, black poplars, among which, when the blackbird ceases to sing, the dove is ready to start up. The bridge they say is Roman is a long way off, but you can cross the river here by twenty twinned stepping-stones, and quite likely the traveller will find the turtle-dove which was drinking there takes fright and flies off. The opposite bank is a rough cliff, and the road has to find its way laboriously until it reaches the top of that black wall, after which it can race off happily across the Beiral plain, which stretches out to the right of the Bernardines' oakwoods, and enjoys the sweet elegance of the birches as they shimmer their reflections into the quiet pools. From the battlements of Belvís, I could see smoke rise from a distant chimney: it was the inn at Termar, where I went to work for a time, before settling to the job of ferryman at Pacios. Those will be other skeins of wool to wind, other memories to breathe life into again, other mirrors in which to inspect oneself, other ways of getting to know the people who come and go through these tales; that is, along this road.

Termar was first a hostel for pilgrims, run by the Bernardine monks of the nearby abbey; their arms can still be seen, surrounded by scallop-shells, set over the door. The abbey stood derelict after the monks departed, and it was a ruin when Señor Morán re-roofed it and opened a shop and an inn there, in order to profit from the fact that the Lugo stage-coach changed horses there. They called it Mesón do Castellano then, a name it still bears; and since on the fourteenth of each month livestock was traded at the place, there grew up the Fair of the Fourteenth, which became very famous. This is held in an attractive grove, the greater part of the field being encircled by laurel, as is the custom of the country, and there are two springs with abundant water. Señor Morán sought a wife in his home region, and the three children of the marriage followed their father's calling. A Portuguese built houses for them beside the inn, and lots of Leonese came to settle, so that the place now considers itself a town of some importance. But I can remember when on that rise in the ground, much exposed to gales, the only building was the pilgrims' hostel. You could always find in the Termar oakwood an early cuckoo and a tawny owl making doom-laden pronouncements. Ah, Termar! The two springs join to make a stream, which while still hardly out of boyhood is made to do a man's work as a miller. And all the birds of Beiral, especially in summer, tuneful song-thrushes, gather in the laurel hedge. When I went to Termar as assistant to the Cistercian abbot, people still talked about the monks of older times, of pilgrims who were generous with alms, of mad Counts who dashed hither and thither propelled by some inner fury, of miracles wrought at the nearby church of San Cosme de Galgao, of ghosts which haunted the old inn ... It seems still that shadowy beings awaken and join me at the door with the arms of Meira over it, up here on the rising ground at Termar: shades which as they come close take on a fleshly covering for an instant, and gather round the fireplace of Lis stone, in which there crackle, in the form of blue, red, and yellow flames, the tales of times long past.

CHAPTER 15

The Greek Dwarf

'The Dwarf is dead, long live the Dwarf!' cried Don Munio the Abbot, drawing a tiny dwarf, a truly miniscule little man, out of his hood. He was dressed as a Bernardine monk, and had a round pink face with his hair cut in a fringe on his forehead, tiny dark but lively eyes, and a body as graceful as that of a Florentine puppet. The abbot placed him on the table, where-upon the dwarf bowed elegantly to the monks and the pilgrims who were spending that May night in the place, and with a little voice which sounded like a silver wire rather than anything human, he began to recount details of his people and his history and how he had come to enter the Cistercian Order.

'So far as the generality of my family goes, I'm a bit taller than the minimum height for recruits in the dwarf army. My male relatives and I among them traditionally serve as pages to the Patriarch of Constantinople's peacocks, and our women as embroiderers in the style they call "the Adana stitch" in the Levant, which as you know is all done with air, one stitch over another enclosing a mirror formed by the orient of a pearl. One younger brother of mine was so small that the Archpriest of As Blanquernas disguised him as a blackbird picking away at a bunch of Catalan grapes on the day of Our Lady's birth, which is when we Greeks start our grape harvest.'

He spat, and went on, 'According to one view which has strong support, and has often been defended with powerful arguments, we descend from Samanian royalty, and are in our present dwarfish state on account of an enamoured poet called Firadusi of the Roses. This bard, who was able, with one line of verse, to produce water out of the air in the dryness of the desert, once saw two little boys playing with an orange in a garden in Damascus, the way lovers play with the moon, and expressed his fervent hope that the boys should never grow out of that happy day, that age of contentment. Hey presto! the wish was granted: the boys never outgrew their childish stature or the joyous merriment of that day, and when they married they bred the whole tribe of my race. With political troubles down the ages the Samanian realm was scattered to the winds, and my ancestors came to rest in Antioch, converted to Christianity, and then moved to Constantinople because the Basileus was curious to acquaint himself with our little tribe which could have fitted all together into a basket of Smyrna figs. At Byzantium we worked at first on curling the Emperor's beard, which as is well known is done to the musical-scale pattern; we climbed about in it to head-butt him, and we worked painting the little fingernails of the empresses and princesses too, this being one of the elegant luxuries that their Isaurian ladyships indulged in. There was one Empress, by name Lady Archipas, who on one of her nails had a painting – you had to view it through a magnifying glass – of the Emperor and his suite going from the palace to the Hippodrome, with the streets full of Blues and Greens shouting away, and all the palace staff with their fancy hats and rods of office and train-bearers, while on another nail she had a pheasant-hunting scene in Colchis, with the imperial hawks flying over a wood decked in autumn colours. But then, as fashions changed, we had to look for new jobs.'

The dwarf, being a student of ancient eloquence, had a thoroughly elegant, well-turned style of narrating. He took from under his scapulary a tiny silver cup, no bigger than a thimble, and dipped it into the Abbot's huge goblet, which was full of red Valdeorras wine. The dwarf took a draught and then went on with his tale:

'Princess Macarea – on whose personal staff I figured as assistant flautist and pusher of her swing – had a very pretty little mouse, white, with three black marks on the tip of its tail. The mouse had the run of the whole palace and went everywhere it wanted, but when it seemed to be lost they sent for me, and I would whistle a tune, whereupon the mouse would come running up to its mistress while she was still wiping away the tears from her blue eyes. This happened hundreds of times, and both the princess and the mouse enjoyed the game. Then came the occasion when the mouse did not answer my whistle. Alarmed, I scoured the palace, and even whistled in the throne-room, where someone told me he had been seen in the garden. I rushed out and whistled among the red tulips, and then a guard at the gates called out that the mouse had gone off prancing about behind a drummer. Still whistling, I crossed the Strait and then the whole of Greece. News came that he had been seen in Mostar and then in Salzburg, but I went on my way and entered Rome: he had been seen crossing the Tiber by the bridge where the Pope has his castle. I spotted him myself in Siena, in the main square, where he did something rather rude under his tail, and then I chased him across France and Navarre, where I picked up a report from some pilgrims who had seen him in a cheese in Villalón de Campos, so I guessed he was heading for Compostela, and yesterday it was my great joy to see him again munching a chestnut in the shade of a birch-tree on the bank of your river. The poor little fellow was quite skinny, and his fur lacked that splendid shine which the princess used to give him with a pomade of Armenian milk. I whistled our game-tune to him once more, but it sounded – doubtless because I was aware of how grieved my mistress was feeling – more like a funeral dirge than a merry dance tune. Anyway, he heard me, and came up to me, but he playfully did one bounce too many, slipped, and fell into the river, where he disappeared into that big eddy by the willows. Now I've resolved to stay here, in your house, as a servant of your lord the Abbot, and I'll write to the Basileus to tell him about this misfortune, and that I hardly dare return to see the tear-filled eyes of my mistress Princess Macarea. What is the name of the river in which the mouse was drowned, please? I shall need to put it in the letter.'

'This river', said Father Abbot, 'is the Miño, and it rises close

by here. This Christian part of the world is Galicia, and we're a
few steps from the road to Santiago.'

The dwarf wiped away a tear, and crept into his hiding-place
in the Abbot's hood, there to nurse his grief.

CHAPTER 16

The Page-Boy of Avignon

'This dwarf person', said a lad who had been sitting listening very attentively to the tale of the mouse, so attentively that he had let a dish of bacon and eggs get cold, 'made the pilgrimage to Santiago without realizing it, and my guess is that he covered most of the distance out of a secret love for the distant princess with the blue eyes, Macarea by name. But I'm making the journey knowing full well what I'm doing, all the way from papal Avignon, in order to ask the Saint to let me, be it just one time more in this life, gaze upon the pale face of another princess, equally remote and just as lovely. This lady of mine is called Anglor, and she lives in a river.'

The boy was about eighteen, very good-looking, tanned by the sun along his lengthy pilgrimage, with his hair cut in a fringe across his forehead in the style of the lay-brethren of St Paul, or 'foundling's toupee' as they call it. He was dressed in the Provençal mode, with bright colours and a loose red cape over them. His aquiline nose was perhaps on the large side, but he had a lot of wit in his grey eyes and his smiling, friendly mouth. He said his name was François, his nickname Pichegru.

'Love comes most often in the twinkling of an eye. Mine began that way, one midsummer night, to be precise last year. I left the lay-brethren to become page-boy to a canon of Avignon, who liked to stroll about on the bridge on a night such as that to watch the lively, motley throng, and especially to listen to the drums, this being a kind of music in which the canons of Avignon, like those of Tarrascon, have always been expert. I was walking a couple of paces behind him, with the parasol folded under my arm: it was an Italian *ombrella* of green silk, and I carried it in case the river should decide to let its waters bloom that night with airy lilies of mist – the canon, you see, blamed the mists of the Rhône for what he called the concomitant flux, which is just about the worst thing that can afflict a nose's mucus. My master paused to watch a Dalmatian who was skilfully juggling with little burning boxes, when he felt the first puff of mist in the air of that midsummer night, and ordered me to put up the umbrella. The moment I opened it there fell from inside the silk, as a rose might fall from a vase, a most lovely maid covered only by the dress of her blushes, her flowing golden hair, and a band of gold on her left knee. Everyone on the bridge stood amazed, the Dalmatian let his fiery boxes go out, and people started to laugh at my master the canon, seeing the girl at his side near-naked as she was. My master got very angry and taking his stand upon the hot embers of his fury started to fire off bits of Bolognese canon law, each of them containing an anathema against those who were mocking his tonsure. The maiden, now wrapped in a cloak provided by the beadle of the Pope's head mustard-mixer, who had happened to be passing, called for silence and exclaimed, "Stop this nonsense! A year ago I came to the bridge to play in the mist, and hid in his Worship the Canon's umbrella just to see how green Neapolitan silk suited me. That was precisely at the moment his page-boy closed it, and I was trapped inside; I had to wait for the same night this year to recover my freedom and my proper form, and I have this only on midsummer night, being the rest of the time water passing under this bridge of Avignon. Behold Anglor, princess of the river!"

'Saying this, she threw off the beadle's cloak and dived through the misty shadows into the water. She left me sighing with love for her, poor wretch that I am. When no-one was looking I used to sniff the umbrella, scented with jasmine and Genoese rose-water as it was, and I wrote lovesongs on bits of coloured paper which I dropped in the river in the hope that the passing waves might read them, the waves being fortunate foamy constituents of her body . . . There were moments when it seemed I could hear, from the willows on the bank, from the murmur of the placid Rhône, the echo of words from my song.' The lad stopped in order to blow his nose with a big yellow handkerchief, the sort they call 'scented with two herbs', but I thought that rather than wiping his nose he was drying his tears. In a voice clouded with grief, he went on, 'I spent my days on the bridge and the river-banks, neglecting to make my master's cocoa, put a shine on his silver buckles, put the white wine to cool, and grease his shotgun ... leaving all my duties till next day. Anglor did not reappear this midsummer night. Perhaps she'll never reappear! Fearing that might indeed be the sad outcome, and that I may never see her again, I am on the pilgrimage to St James. On the way I amuse myself teaching this thrush to sing a sad little tune I composed in Sahagún, when I stayed at the inn there. When the bird knows it really well I'll set him free so that he can act as singing-master to other thrushes, and then all the birds of the air can sing it. The whole world will know then how much page-boy François, better known as Pichegru in the ancient city of Avignon in Provence, the city with the famous bridge, loves and always will love his Anglor, princess of the river.'

The page-boy rose from his stool and went out of the hostel to take a stroll along the road. The tame thrush began to fill the air with Pichegru's lovesong.

'It's easy to see', said a tailor from Zamora who was on the pilgrimage too, 'that the fellow really is in love, or he wouldn't have left the bacon and eggs on his plate.'

I can still imagine myself back in Termar as it's getting dark, observing page-boy Pichegru walking in the drizzle without noticing how soaked he's getting, with his head bowed and the wind blowing his loose red cloak around him.

CHAPTER 17

The Huguenot of Riol

Concerning the table at which the pilgrims dined at Termar, it was said that it bore a bloodstain which no-one had been able to remove, even by planing the wood down, since the fresh blood had soaked the whole thickness of the cherrywood plank. I heard this from the carpenter who came to Miranda to make the new stairway up to the attic and put the floor into the rear part of the loft. His name was Master Felpeto, and Don Merlin valued him highly, for he was a famous craftsman, numbering among his achievements the making of the oaken tricycle for Don López Borricón, Bishop of Mondoñedo, the one who when the first Carlist war broke out abandoned his see in order to go off to the Basque Provinces and listen to the rightful king's cannons firing away. The Bishop was given to riding the contraption along the paths in the episcopal garden, with an acolyte standing on the axle of the rear wheels blowing a whistle in order to warn his nephews, servants and familiars to get out of the way, since His Grace was coming at full speed. Anyway, back to our bloodstain. It gave rise to many different opinions. Some of the more erudite monks maintained that it was a mark left by an Innocent of Bethlehem who was on the pilgrimage to Compostela, since other Innocents had left similar marks in the Great Charterhouse; also in Palermo, in a Franciscan house. They added that this Innocent had left a bloodstain not only on the table at which he sat, but also on the bread he ate and the cup from which he drank. Others held that possibly an unknown pilgrim had been murdered there one dark night, and that it was time to report this in Lugo so that the authorities could investigate. The occasional bright spark, who brought up the signs left by the Wandering Jew, was not lacking; and others who said (insisting that they really knew all about it) that ever since the Catalans in Pontedeume and the Leonese had been making wine in Galicia, such marks were common on tables in inns and hostelries. It really was blood, however, human blood, and I'll tell you the true story of it, just as it was once told to me by the secularized monk of Goás, Don Ernestino Tejada, once when he was passing through Pacios – where I was ferryman – on his way to Lugo, where he was to present some pickled chickens to a magistrate from his own Riojan region. He was a preaching fellow always on the move from here to there on some such business!

One year in France, 1572 to be precise – I can assure you this is right, because I have it in print in an instalment of the *Defence of Ravaillac's Crime*, the crime being that this Ravaillac stabbed a most Christian monarch through and through, some said to stop his whoring, others (the majority) because he was a heretic and an enemy of Holy Church. Now in this same year 1572, in early September, in the sea just off Asturias, about where the Navia river runs out, some seamen from Luarca found a boat drifting. In it a badly wounded man lay close to death: he was a young gentleman belonging to that heathen sect in Médoc, a fanatical Huguenot who had fled from the massacre which Catherine de' Medici, who then ruled in France, had unleashed on St Bartholomew's day against the adherents of the Protestant Reformation. The seamen carried him to the manor-house at Riol, whose garden goes right down to the shore, but he died just two hours later, still loyal to his religion, crying out for vengeance and cursing Queen Catherine. So obstinate was the Huguenot, so bitter the gall of his anger and so strong his partisan feelings, that he seemed to find no repose in death, for each year on the eve of St Bartholomew's day he appears in the main drawing-room of the house, goes over to the balcony, and resting his right hand on one of the window-panes leaves a mark there. The gentleman disappears there next to the balcony, but the fresh, warm blood stains the glass ... So it went on year after year until a French clergyman who was going to Compostela carrying letters from the French Gaston de Isaba family for relatives of his in Oscos and Taramundi, among whom are the Ibáñez people of Sargadelos who make the fine china, stayed at Riol. The tonsured Frenchman was overcome by compassion for the Huguenot, whose castle and vineyard were very close to his own home, and for the suffering he was undergoing on account of his heretical pride. It occurred to him to offer the Huguenot to the Apostle, and he spent the days that led up to the feast of St Bartholomew trying to work out how he might make such an offering. It was not easy to see how he could take the ghost, who after all was a wandering soul, with him to Compostela. After racking his brains it occurred to him to collect the blood which the heretic left on the glass – usually enough, according to witnesses, to fill a glass of the sort you have anisette in – in a phial of Murano crystal, in which he carried about a supply of essence of peppermint (this being a sovereign remedy for headaches). The French priest would appear with this blood in Compostela, and beg the Apostle to pardon the offender. Such was the plan of the good abbé, whose name was Laffite, and he carried out the first part of it. He was a fat, peasanty sort of person, sparing with his Latin, thickly bearded, in no way resembling the French abbés who appeared in the novels read by the dwarf and the young Countesses at Belvís. This Father Laffite was of the older kind, rather countrified, a hunting and wine-making cleric, skilled at fattening young turkeys up for Christmas, and much sought-after in the Guyenne region to preach the sermon on the Descent from the Cross.

On the eve of St Bartholomew, the Reverend Father Laffite knelt down by the balcony to await the appearance of the Huguenot. He was as punctual as an English clock striking twelve. He was dressed precisely as the sailors had found him in his boat, but his face was now wreathed in a sort of shiny mist. The apparition went over to the balcony and placed his right hand against the glass: he seemed to be looking out into the night and listening to the dull roar of the sea, then suddenly the luminous mist was swirling all around, before merging with the darkness. The priest got up at once and began to sop up the blood with a piece of lint, the squire of Riol helping him with a teaspoon; they could see that the blood did not coagulate but remained fresh and liquid. Father Laffite set off next day, and after resting a bit in Lourenzá where the Benedictine monks made a great fuss of him, he arrived on his Poitevin mule – this breed is a placid, good-tempered one, because the Poitou jackass has a lymphatic temperament and is none too quick in the business of covering mares, even needing, at times, to be urged on by singing to him – at the Termar inn.

For political reasons a certain Salamancan named Jovito Bejarano, who had been a guerrilla fighter of Julián el Charro's, and one of whose brothers was a Bernardine monk, had at the time sought refuge in Meira. He was in the habit of going along to the Termar inn at supper-time to see if some stranger dropped in, even though there were in truth few enough of these then because of the troubles. In an incidental way his Salamancan stallion wrought havoc with the abbey's mares, to the fury of the lay-brother in charge of the stable. That's the fellow from Betanzos who was later in charge of the Curtis stagecoach, and got nicknamed 'Old Slowcoach'. Jovito was at Termar when the reverend Frenchman arrived: they got drinking together, the priest explaining to the guerrilla fighter all about the revolution in France and the adventures of Napoleon. When they found out that they shared high Catholic views they sealed their agreement with a jar of Chantada wine, and the priest revealed that he was carrying the Huguenot's blood in the Murano phial and was going to pray to St James to save his soul from damnation. Jovito asked to see the phial and Father Laffite showed it to him with pleasure, drawing his attention to the fact that the blood was fresh and liquid, whereupon the Salamancan guerrilla-fighter exclaimed, 'This can't be any miracle to do with Huguenoteries! It's the power of a faithful Catholic sword that pierced the hide of that diabolical Frenchy!'

All in one instant as Jovito said this, fire burst out in the little bottle and the Murano crystal shattered in his hand. The Salamancan went deathly white, and stared at the blood which had fallen on the table, more flame than blood and now burning the wood.

'Some foul temper that heretic had!' cried Jovito, recovering somewhat.

Father Laffite fell to his knees and prayed, closing his eyes, for the soul of the impenitent heretic.

CHAPTER 18

The Portuguese Cock

I always heard my master Don Merlin speak of the ancient city of Braga with great respect. Don Esmeraldino da Cámara Mello de Lima, Viscount Ribeirinha, a distinguished Portuguese gentleman of the highest nobility and more than ample wealth, and a native of the city, had fine rooms in a big house in the Rúa dos Confidentes there. I heard tell from one of the liveried servants who was in charge of his shotguns that this Viscount Esmeraldino was the handsomest man in all Portugal in his time, with fetching beauty-spots and such a sad look in his wide dark eyes that it was as though when he rested his gaze on you for a time a mist of gentle caresses emerged from under the fluttering silk of his long eyelashes to wrap you around. By means of this gaze alone he aroused strong passions, aided too by the fact that he was on the short side, had most elegant movements, and was moreover generous and free with valuable presents. He brought Parisian fashions to Braga, in respect of dress, especially waistcoats, and of dances, and of hair-styles and parlour-games too, and he even brought fashionable words when he came back from France, such as *sentimental*, *bombón*, *nenúfar*, even *la merde latine* and *le doré aux cochons*. These last were expressions – begging your pardon – for use about the clergy and the archbishop, respectively (maybe I remember these because they were much used in revolting liberal circles in those insurrectional times). But all these fine points and charming features which Don Esmeraldino had in his gentlemanly person served him only to break the sixth Commandment, a business in which he was both active and regular. In order to keep the tally of his conquests he had a piece of wrought iron nailed over the door of the house with a mahogany board hung from it, on

which he cut a cross with his penknife each time he triumphed
in Venus's lists. The people of Braga thought this was splendid.
They took to following the Viscount around, discussing which
lady might be next to capitulate, and whether it was a lavish
present or real love that caused it. Everyone claimed to be able
to hear secret serenades, and the whole of Braga was alive with
wishful witnesses and false reports about maidens dishonoured
and husbands whose horns fitted them all too well, all so
detailed that no qualified lawyer's clerk could have done better
on official paper.

Viscount Ribeirinha was perfectly happy with this life-style,
famed throughout Portugal as a great lover, when there arrived
in Braga an Italian opera company, whose chief adornment was
the prima donna Signorina Carla, a blonde who wore low-cut
dresses and sang like a lark. Don Esmeraldino, who had his own
box with his coat of arms over it, had himself introduced to her
in the theatre at the first performance. Now Signorina Carla was
very fond of jewels, and once Don Esmeraldino had set all the
jewellers in Portugal to work for him, the lady was able to show
off a whole display-case of gems every night. The Viscount took
the lovely lady about in his coach, from the Suiza Hotel to the
theatre and back again, and he even had the coach upholstered
in green, for that was her favourite colour and her eyes were
green too. There were guitar concerts under the soprano's
window, afternoon teas in the Viscount's garden, and lots of
other elegant attentions. Braga hardly slept at all, since everyone
was constantly going along to inspect the mahogany board to
see if a new cross had been cut in honour of Venus. Even today
it is rumoured, when there is talk of this, that the lad who acted
as cup-bearer to the Cathedral canons went along privily to see
if the amorous contest had come to any conclusion, so that he
could inform the Penitentiary who was composing a special
sermon against this new Don Juan. Then came the final performance by the Italian company in Braga – a piece entitled *Looking
for Love* – and off they went to Oporto. Don Esmeraldino bade
farewell to Signorina Carla, kissing her hand and making her a

present of a fan with golden ribs, and then he stood in the middle of the street waving her goodbye with a green handkerchief until the coach turned into Adro da Canela. Accompanied by his friends Don Esmeraldino walked home slowly, talking merrily the while: he said goodnight to his friends and paused on the pavement, before going up to his rooms, with half Braga there in the Rúa dos Confidentes agog with curiosity. Viscount Ribeirinha handed his stick to a servant, took his penknife out of the pocket of his green waistcoat (green as the eyes of the singing Signorina), and cut a cross – much bigger and more elaborate than usual – on the mahogany board. Those present applauded just as if they had been in the theatre.

The news raced all round Portugal, and the Lusitanian courtliness of Don Esmeraldino was widely praised, since he had waited till Carla's departure before publishing the fact that there had been what His Honour the judge of Abadín called 'some degree of personal intimacy'. The House of Nobles held a special session and resolved to pay tribute to such exceptional chivalry, worthy of past times, and a deputation – led by a Marquis who at Evora had achieved among Andalusian and Portuguese ladies nearly the same tally as Don Esmeraldino in his town – set off from Lisbon for Braga. The old aristocracy of the city preferred not to attend the homage ceremony, in order to avoid gossip, but all the common sort of people were in festive mood in the streets and squares. Don Esmeraldino served light refreshments to the peers, people down in the street cheered, and the titled folk decided to come out onto the balcony to acknowledge the applause. Don Esmeraldino went pale with the emotion of the moment, so the Marquis of Evora, thinking it proper to give way to the Viscount's higher rank, took off his top hat with its three buckles and shouted, 'Two primates now in Braga! I give you the Cock of Portugal!'

At that very moment Don Esmeraldino turned red, blue, and yellow, burst open like a rocket taking off, and changed into a rooster, a very fine bird with a noble crest and magnificent tail. He flew from one balcony to another and finally perched on the wrought-iron bar from which, like the sign outside an English pub, there swung the board which bore the complete tally of crosses marking victories in contests of love. The peers stood aghast, the common folk rushed about shouting, women fainted, a Franciscan cried out that such was the proper punishment for so much sinfulness, and then one of Don Esmeraldino's nephews was able to catch the bird and pop him in a cage. The Penitentiary brought his sermon forward a month in order to emphasize what a fate awaited the supporters of free fornication. We can be sure, as Don Esmeraldino's liveried servant – the one who looked after his shotguns – told me, that Portugal virtually went into mourning: there were hardly any serenades, the women didn't look so attractive, and we may sum it up by saying that in Braga alone two perfumeries had to close.

With Don Esmeraldino in a very handsome cage, the doctors came to see him, as did the exorcist from Viseu. They undertook every possible kind of test, but the only one who seemed to come near a solution was the Quintadinha tailor, a famous bonesetter, who considered that to keep the cockerel happy and in good shape while consultations proceeded it would be best to keep the bird in a larger cage and to hang the mahogany board with the crosses on it so that it could swing to and fro. Now Don Esmeraldino had a Hieronymite half-brother in the severe house which these penitents pleasurably occupy in Lisbon, a man of great learning who, while leafing through an ancient tome, came across two cases in which a man had turned into a bird: the remedy lay in a pilgrimage to Santiago, where it was well known that such beings in the feathered state had been restored to their original form. The family agreed to offer Don Esmeraldino to the Apostle, and thus it was that one day there appeared in Termar: the Hieronymite on his mule; Don Esmeraldino's liveried servant and shotgun specialist on a rather nervy bay horse; the cage on a litter, together, that is, with two boys to carry the litter; two more servants in reserve; and – in order to draw up a true account of what happened on the pilgrimage – His Worship the Ecclesiastical Fiscal of Braga, as recording clerk. I never saw such a tall man on such a tiny mule, his feet so close to the ground as he rode that he could have played football with the stones on the road.

In Termar there gathered to see Don Esmeraldino in cock form half the Cistercians from the Meira monastery and all the householders and servants: he was an exceptionally handsome rooster with his bright multicoloured plumage, most of it like old gold in sunlight, his spurs splendid, and his blood-red crest with its five points erect, and he was in good voice too, fluent and untiring. From the roof of his cage there hung the mahogany board with the crosses, swinging away; the younger monks began to count the crosses and the cock seemed to join in by crowing loudly as each number was called. When one of the page-boys went to change his water and serve him a chopped-up egg, he opened the cage door a bit too wide and the cockerel took his chance to escape – swift as any arrow fired at the battle of Solferino – from his painted wickerwork prison. He flew up to the main beam of the dining-room, leaped from there to the back of the Fiscal's mule, and from there out through the open door into the countryside. We all shot out in pursuit of the bird, the monks drawing up their skirts, a lay-brother imitating a hen's cackle, the Hieronymite praying, the Fiscal fanning himself with his hat, and the householders, the servants, and I laughing at it all and amazed at this turn of events. The cock set off for the Abbey of Meira, flew over the walls of the old yard, and when we caught up with him, there he was strutting proudly among the hens, as much of a Sultan as the Turk of Constantinople in his harem. If it were possible for a cockerel to carry a penknife in his waistcoat and cut Burgundian crosses on a mahogany board, Don Esmeraldino would have been at the job, lest his memory of the total should fail him . . .

When we caught the bird he was returned to his cage, and the procession designed to undo the spell continued to Santiago. The news we had in Meira and Termar was that Don Esmeraldino caught a cold in Melide and that two wens the size of Verín onions (if you'll pardon the comparison) came out on his crop, followed by a sabbatine fever; this finished him off, and he gave up the ghost in a Santiago inn. The general opinion is that he was buried in a yard there, resting on the mahogany board. Today there's a race of golden fowls in Meira and Azúmara, great layers and very good in chicken fricassee. People call them the Portuguese breed, since they are evidently the result of the short time Don Esmeraldino spent in the old yard of the ever-illustrious Royal Abbey of Santa María de Meira. My Don Merlin would have loved to be principal consultant in this strange case!

CHAPTER 19

M'sieur Tabarie's Tale

Je luy donne ma librairie,
Et le Romman du Pet au Diable,
Lequel maistre Gui Tabarie
Grossoya, qu'est hom veritable.
Par cayers est soubz une table.
Combien qu'il soit rudement faict,
La matière est si très notable,
Qu'elle amende tout le meffaict.

François Villon, *Grand Testament*

This summer I came across – the river was running low, people
and cattle could get dry-shod across the Valiña ford, my boat
was tied up to its mooring-post in Padrón for over a month, and
I had lots of time to take it easy at home – as I was saying, I
came across two instalments of *The Tale of The Devil's Fart*
which Alsir the Moor had left with me. As I read, wearing the
spectacles I now need to use all the time, I laughed a good deal,
and now I think it would be a good idea to pass on the gist of
the story. The daemon in question, Cobillon by name, came to
our attention in Miranda when my master had to go to Gaul to
banish the stink of sulphur from a county in that realm; at first
it was thought that a mine had been accidentally broken into,
but it turned out that it was caused only by a band of daemons
which Lucifer, the head devil, had ordered to be released over
England, and which had left in that county, in a cave, its old
clothes. With the stink that hung about those old rags you could
have sulphurized half Ribeiro. Now this Cobillon was a rather
elegant daemon, who had studied perfumery in Florence, Italy,
where he got into the habit of bathing in frangipani water. The

story goes that in Soria there was a young widow who was a great devotee of St Cyriac, and since she had a good income of her own and had inherited even more from her late husband, she proposed to build a chapel in the saint's honour on a hillside where the witches of the country round about Osma were wont to spend the hottest part of the summer. These women brought in a decently white Aragonese daemon to turn the widow away from her notion, but she speedily found out that it was a daemon that was tempting her, for she had a very keen sense of smell and could instantly fix any nasty odour that was passing. The search was then on throughout Satandom for a daemon that didn't stink of sulphur and smelled more or less human, and the one they lit on was Cobillon, who at the time was in Paris making French ladies smell nice. The widow had already contracted builders for the hermitage, so it was urgent to upset her plans. Cobillon went to Soria, then, very smartly dressed, and introduced himself as a relative of a good Sorian family. He went around leaving tips and distributing alms, and put it about that as luck would have it he had in his pocket a phial containing water distilled from St Cyriac's beard. It took only a moment for the widow to hear of this and to invite the imp to tea. Cobillon turned up in a green frock-coat and carrying a silver-topped cane, with a gold watch-chain in his waistcoat, and hanging from it, the phial with St Cyriac's water. The widow – naturally enough – fell in love on the instant with the handsome fellow, who immediately allowed her to sniff the phial and promised to dye a hairy spot she had under her chin with Maltese chamomile, and he invited her there and then to go off with him to Tarragona, where he had his town house and where his chaplain, who was a cousin of the Archbishop's, would marry them. Doña Florinda, for that was the widow's name, asked for a day in which to prepare her answer, to which Cobillon readily agreed. But during that day a woman who had been nursemaid to the deceased husband when he was a baby and happened to be in the house whispered to the widow that her suitor could be another daemon. Doña Florinda assured herself that she could smell only roses, frangipani water and Polo toilet-water on her suitor, for she was so eager to marry that her flesh (and very good flesh it was too, splendid, white, and luscious) was all a-tingle with the prospect. None the less she racked her brains trying to think of a way to uncover the deception, if deception there were. Cobillon, concealed in the fireplace, overheard the conversation between the widow and the nursemaid, and resolved to deploy the whole battery of his perfumes in order not to give himself away. He bathed in frangipani water, washed his feet with lily-scented blotting-paper, smarmed his hair with rose-honey, and finally to sweeten his breath drank a flask of nard wine. The widow told Cobillon about the white daemon, and how the witches were going about upsetting her plans for the chapel dedicated to St Cyriac, and about her fear of being tempted by the chief devil and his gang of horned henchmen. With tears in her eyes, and asking his pardon because he was such a passionate man, the widow begged Cobillon to be so kind as to break wind so that she could determine what he smelled of. Cobillon was reluctant, but the widow went on tearfully beseeching, and since Cobillon assumed that the aromatic wine he had drunk must by now be in his nether regions, he gathered his strength and fired off a huge explosive fart, which echoed round his tight breeches like a drum-roll on a parade-ground. The whole room filled with the sweetest possible aroma of flowery nard, at which the widow flung herself into Cobillon's arms. The imp carried her off in his coach to Tarragona, with two chests containing the widow's gold up in the luggage-rack. They had the archiepiscopal towers of the city in sight when Cobillon between kisses asked Doña Florinda to see what she thought of a new perfume, and right there under her so sensitive nose he breathed out a cloud of sulphur, shouting that she had been sharing her bed with an evil – if learned – spirit. The widow died there and then in the coach, of sheer grief, and Cobillon went back to Paris with the gold and resumed his perfumery business.

I like to retell this tale because it was the first I ever read. My master liked me to tell it too, especially after we had had chestnut soup for lunch. When I got to the bit about the fart I always said 'If you'll pardon the expression' and bowed to the company. I tell it too so that you can see what a good time we had in Miranda during the winter, when it was snowy and the water blocked the road across the meadows, and the dogs barked at the wolf that passed close by the houses even in daylight. I'd love to live those times again!

Paul et Virginie

Reading a novel called *Paul et Virginie* was all the rage in Paris. I hope I recall correctly that it was by a tonsured gentleman, Don Bernardin de Saint-Pierre. Elimas the Arab on one of his visits to us sold a copy to the girls at Belvís. At the time Don Merlin wasn't living at Miranda any more; Xosé do Cairo was looking after the house, and had just married one of the young Countesses, the one with the blondest hair who had an affair with the young Belmonte heir and had a stillborn baby. I went up there one afternoon to pay a call and ask permission to chop down a couple of willows on Don Merlin's land, which prevented the carts that were heading for the ferry at Pacios from turning round. It was all set down in a book that Don Merlin kept: the list of the Miranda properties and their bounds, the rights of way, how much firewood was allowed to be cut for the church at Doncide, which days were allowed at Os Cabos and Pontigo for water for irrigation and for the mill, and the fact that those two willows were called respectively Pablo and Virginia. This was one of my master's whims, attaching names drawn from stories to inanimate objects, an aspect of his consideration and feelingness of mind: he called his shotgun Napoli, his gig Phaeton, the eddy in the Miño where the Persian imp Pinto's boat turned over Salamina, and so on. Once, when he was travelling to Lugo or to France, and was bringing some handsome present back for Lady Guinevere, he told me in his affectionate way to dress up a bit and take the present in to her on a tray, clapping me on the back and remarking, 'Take this most distinguished offering to her Ladyship Dulcinea del Toboso.'

As he said this his broad smile would be clouded by a fleeting shadow of sadness. You could tell that Merlin had always been more than a little in love with her. Anyway, back to our willows, which were weeping ones, and in rather a bad state. Xosé do Cairo gave me the permission I needed to cut them down, but his wife intervened and begged me not to do it, out of respect for the tragic memory of the two lovers Paul and Virginie, whose story she had read so often at Belvís, weeping the while, and especially when she was pregnant by the young Belmonte heir, when reading about the misfortunes of the enamoured couple consoled her somewhat in her own sorry state. Xosé do Cairo decided that her wish should be respected. I think personally that he did it because although she was his wife she was also a lady of the aristocratic Belvís Castle stock, whereas if he had been married as I was to a serving-wench he would have laughed at her tearful pleading and told me to go ahead and chop the two trees, lovers' names and all, right down. It was a habit of Xosé's to dismiss women's delicate feelings and finicky whims as so much whorish wheedling!

I accepted another glass and asked the young Countess what the story of Paul and Virginie was all about. She burst into tears and said she couldn't bear to tell me in case, in reviving the memory of those tragic events, her milk might dry up (she was still suckling Leonardín, quite big though he was now; he was born two months after their marriage). Now I remember what her Ladyship the Countess's name was: Martina. She got another jar of wine for us and went off to get on with the housework.

'Martina read this story to me when I went to start courting her at Belvís, avoiding the dwarf on the way,' Xosé do Cairo remarked, 'and if you're still keen to hear about it, we'll finish this jar and I'll see if I can remember all the ins and outs, and then I'll see if I can spell it out to you. We're not bothered about our milk drying up, are we, and even if we were, it wouldn't do any harm to any third party.' We drank that jar down in silence, and cheered ourselves up with another. Xosé then told me the tale of Paul and Virginie, shortening it a bit here and there, and asking my pardon for any lapses on his part, since it was the first time he'd tried to tell a story that had real literary origins.

'This Paul that figures in the title had loved to sit looking at the vastness of the sea, ever since he was a small child. He sat on the shore and dreamed up routes across the sea, following them out a long way, imagining that here might be an island, and there a meeting with a brig and a girl on the deck waving goodbye with her handkerchief, then closer in a huge steady lighthouse beacon burning away in the darkness, then away to the right fearful squally winds, to the left a school of immense blue whales. Then at the end of his voyage he'd find a land of innocence, one where animals talked, there was no notion of personal property, the prettiest of the girls fell instantly in love with the newly-arrived stranger, and at the door of every house there was a tree that provided bread and another that gave wine. After reading Bouffon on plants and animals he could duly populate his islands and countries. However, all this thinking and imagining – it's the same thing, really – made him restless and out of sorts: he was dissatisfied with his country, ill at ease with his family, his work, his friends, even with day and night. He became so restless that he resolved to set sail one Easter in a three-master that was leaving Honfleur: you remember, Honfleur, where that fellow who called himself an Admiral came from, to ask our master Merlin to remove the spell from a silver fork which turned meat into fish when he ate with it. He told us what a handsome place Honfleur was, with its painted houses, and the taverns underneath, all with little windows and panes of coloured glass, and such elegant inhabitants that even though it was a small place there were two glove-shops, and some of the taverns were for smokers and some for non-smokers. So Paul embarked on the three-master, whose name was *La Bella Corentina*, and sailed off to America to look for the north-west passage, which I would guess in comparison with anything we have here is a really windy spot and a great place for shipwrecks. Paul left France one sunny morning, and thought the land breeze which carried the ship out to sea was a good omen. I won't trouble you with details of the voyage, or the storms, and I don't remember if Paul was sea-sick. Forty-two days out, while Paul was hanging his stockings out to dry from the tip of a spar, he caught a whiff of the distant land, and it was none other than the smell with which he had invested the land of innocence which he had earlier dreamed up. The captain told him that in that direction they wouldn't reach land in a month of sailing, and the sailors, Normans for the most part, laughed at his sense of smell; but there was one man, a Portuguese, who said he had heard that Malacca was fairly close in that direction, once they had found their way through the Guinea strait. Paul went on savouring the smell, feeling almost caressed by it, and he lay absorbing it at night, stretched out like a dog which senses that his master's hand is coming to stroke his back pleasurably. Again overcome by his former restlessness, he decided to steal the ship's dinghy and row until he reached his land of innocence; which he did. In his disturbed state of mind he had given no thought to food supplies, and after two days' rowing there wasn't a crumb left that he hadn't picked out of his pockets, so he was reduced to living off the smell of the land, ever warmer and denser all around him. But he couldn't live any longer on mere yearnings, and at daybreak on the fifth day he fainted away. It seems that a current carried the boat towards the shore, in so kindly a way that it deposited Paul on the sand at the very moment that a girl called Virginie was hunting there for an earring she'd lost. On seeing the fainting youth she called out to the old woman who was with her, Doña Terencia, who on feeling his heart could tell he was still alive, and with a sip of rum and water mixed with sugar they were able to bring him round. The first thing he saw on opening his eyes was Virginie's face, and a sweetly pretty one it was too, if a bit on the dark side. Doña Terencia went off to look for the village policeman, while Virginie stayed with Paul, giving him sips of sugared water and sticks of cinnamon to suck, stroking his brow and uttering encouraging words. Paul was already in love before arriving, truth to tell, because he'd fallen in love in his dreams. Ah, I forgot to tell you: this Virginie was completely naked, with all her attractions on view. His Lordship the Count, my deceased father-in-law, peace be with him, used to say that the worst damage this story of Paul and Virginie did in Paris was that the men by daydreaming and letting their hair go uncombed were imitating Paul, while the women imitated Virginie and seized any chance to undress, with all of which it wasn't surprising that soon after Napoleon got himself cuckolded.'

This was all a lot of narrating for Xosé do Cairo to have to do, and we needed to drink another jar. He rolled himself a cigarette, taking his time, got out his tinder-box and lit up, and after savouring a couple of puffs, he felt strong enough to go on with the tale. He was evidently pleased with the way the story was coming out, and the commentary. I never knew he was so well up with the wide world.

'It took Doña Terencia a while to find the policeman, and Paul used the time to inspect little Virginie closely and fall quite definitely in love. He had a new suit in his bag, consisting of a lacy jacket and tight trousers of blue velvet, with a red silk sash for his waist; with Virginie's aid he stood up and in the most natural way undressed there and then in front of her and went for a swim before donning his new suit, and he didn't go off to relieve himself in private either, since he did not care to cast a shadow of sinfulness over a place where he, both in his earlier imaginings and from what he could now see, could perceive nothing but pleasant natural innocence. (I think he was being a jot too confident about this.) When Doña Terencia and the policeman arrived they found the two youngsters hand in hand, looking into each other's eyes. The policeman – a fat, clean-shaven chap, with a chain of coconut beads round his neck – asked Paul questions in a variety of languages, to which Paul was unable to reply, whereupon the policeman led him to a hut beside a spring and left him there in Doña Terencia's charge with a good stock of food. Virginie stayed with him, to warm his feet and brush the flies off. They spent happy days in the hut, and Paul got used to being innocently naked as the two wandered the woods and the shore teaching each other words, with Doña Terencia helping their love-affair along. On day nine the policeman came back with an order from the ruler of the country that Paul should be brought before him, since the king wished to meet him; it meant a two-day journey, and Virginie wept as the lad was led away. Now the king – here I have to leave a lot out so as to get towards the end – had a daughter who had been born black, and since Paul was so white and fair-skinned, the king had the idea of mating them to see if he could extend the fame of his family by having them produce a child with black and white stripes (there were stories in which the king had had a red grandfather too). Paul allowed himself to be led into this, quite easily, since he had no idea what was going on. So there he was in bed with the black girl, who was a very nice jolly person. Well, Virginie arrived and discovered this new affair; she burst into tears and shot off to the woods, where she was captured by some Indians out hunting, and they sold her to a Dutchman who kept a cut-price store in a bay nearby, where the cod fishermen came ashore to renew their water supplies. Paul saw Virginie run off and, being unguarded, went off after her. The Indians caught him too, and sold him to the black king of Florida, who employed him as a slave to carry him on his shoulders at parties. The Dutchman sold the innocent Virginie, weak with weeping, to an Indian chief who was in the business of fattening women up for the kings of Mexico. I should never get to the end of telling you how Paul changed masters seven times, always on Virginie's track, and how Virginie was four times married against her will, and was ravished away twice, while on the final occasion that she was sold, she returned to the Dutchman's hands. There in his cut-price store she prepared to die, and was weeping away when in walked Paul, he having escaped from his last master, a heavy smoker who adored Havana cigars. The lovers recognized each other, and since Paul now spoke her language, they were able to exchange all manner of sweet nothings and agree to forget about each other's wanderings. Paul explained to Virginie that he had gone unwillingly to the black princess's bed, the proof of this being that the child who was born later emerged black as soot, he not having put the slightest bit of love into the business but merely a lot of hard work. But it was too late for Virginie, who died as she granted him forgiveness, leaving Paul with a baby she'd had by the king of Mexico, lying there at the foot of her bed sucking cinnamon sticks. This, reminding Paul of the sticks he had sucked when Virginie found him on the beach, softened Paul's heart, and he decided not to sell the child to the Dutchman, who would have paid good money because an order had come from Spain for an Indian prince who was needed to appear at some function. Once when we were chatting about all this, the priest at Xemil told me that if the story was true, the order about the child would have been connected with the Barcelona Exhibition, which we saw in the papers was to be declared open by Queen Christine.'

'And what happened to Paul?' I asked.

'He went back to France, with a little bag of gold which he used to establish a shop for maps and telescopes in Honfleur, and he sent the little prince off to school. He consoled himself by watching the ships come and go, and sucking cinnamon sticks. Maybe he found a new wife, since it's not good for a man to be on his own.'

So I went home to Pacios, without being allowed to chop the weeping willows down. In the winter of '92, when the river was in spate, the one called Virginia went off downstream. There was Pablo, all alone next to the ford. When they built the dam on the river at Lañor, the water covered him up.

Miscellaneous Notes Concerning
the Life of Don Merlin,
Magician of Brittonia

Late in May an English gentleman crossed the river in Felipe de Amancia's boat. He was red-haired and short, but in spite of this seemed very stylish and well set-up, and wore an Inverness cape with a green and black check pattern, and on his head a cream-coloured waterproof bowler-hat. He carried a big black leather briefcase under his arm, and told Felipe that he was travelling from Rennes in Brittany to Miranda to inquire whether Don Merlin, in his period of residence in Galicia, had had any children.

'Don Merlin was my master', said Felipe, 'but I've had no news of him for seven years now come St Mark's day. Could he be dead, perhaps?'

'It's less than a year since some Irish clergymen saw him in Naples, in Santa Maria della Grotta. He told them he was there as a pilgrim.'

'He had that notion, yes, of not dying before he had been to Jerusalem.' Felipe crossed himself, without letting go of his punting-pole, so that the tip of it formed the Cross on his face. '*Ad multos annos!* As for any offspring in Miranda, no, he had none. My master used to say that he was celibate for three principal reasons. The first was that he was a philosopher, and Dame Philosophy demands chastity. Concerning this Don Merlin cited as an example a relative of his of former times, Abelard of Paris, who was violently castrated by the servants of that canon whose niece, one Heloïse, he had caused to fall in love with him. That was an awful business. The second reason was obvious when Merlin stated his age, adding that if he were to fall to lustful temptations, he would look for some fifteen-year-old girl, naturally within a fully canonical marriage, which would cause the people to jeer, since they are always on the lookout for old men who marry young girls, and the couple are hardly allowed to leave the church before salacious imaginations start to invent horns for hubby's head. At that point he would read me a letter from the bishop of this diocese, Don Guevara, to Master Rubín of Valencia, an old man who married a young girl, or he would tell the tale of Valls the barber, a surgeon and blood-letting expert of Vinaroz, who at seventy wed a girl of seventeen: he did it only because he liked her to comb and stroke his hair, which he wore long, right down to his shoulders. The girl one day knotted his hair round his neck, and drew it tight. He also used to tell about his friend Fouché, a Frenchman, the most secretive man of his times, to whom Merlin had sold a cipher with which one could write in the dark; when old and weary he married a girl called Ernestine, who cuckolded him. As for the third reason, he never stated it, but struck his breast as though to say *Mea culpa*, and just once I heard him exclaim, "Ah, Felipe, a faithful heart is worth the sun and the moon!" Those of us who served in his house at Miranda think that he spent his years there in love with Lady Guinevere – that most worthy dame, may she rest in peace – damping down whatever fire was in his heart out of the respect owed to the widowed queen, respect which he always showed.'

The Englishman did not seem very convinced, remarking that he followed the methods of the higher schools of thought, and that one would have to take a look at the registers of births in the province and, if it were possible, another look at Merlin's papers. 'Moreover,' he added, 'all that about celibacy imposed by philosophy would have applied to him only in old age, because as a youngster, around the royal courts, your master was pretty quick on the draw.'

The Englishman laughed. He was a man who, although a bit on the haughty side, perhaps because of his lack of height, was polite and courtly in conversation, and a pleasant enough talker. He went to sit at the front of the boat, took his bowler-hat off and placed it on his knees, and taking a comb from his pocket began to comb his thick hair, making two partings, from right to left, in the style that was then called 'the harvest'. His bright little eyes were as lively in their movement as a lizard's tail. 'At the inn I'll tell you one or two ancient bits of information about your master, and I trust that in return you'll favour me with the same about the period that Merlin the Magician spent in retirement here.'

Since Felipe de Amancia was always curious to know more about Merlin's origins, early studies, life, and scientific accomplishments, he accepted the Englishman's invitation with pleasure. The latter introduced himself as Mister James Craven, solicitor and notary public of the city and deanery of Truro in Cornwall, duly qualified by examination, and executor of the will of Baron Galloden, a cousin of Merlin's.

'Ah,' said Felipe, 'I remember my master talking about him, saying that he was a great huntsman, and that he wrote a book in Latin to prove that the earth is not round and there are no antipodes.'

'Yes, that's the man for whom I am executor. He brought good new styles of dress to Wales, as you can see from these winter garments I'm wearing, which he left to me in a holograph codicil. The Inverness cape belonged to a quick-change artist.'

Mister Craven stood up in the middle of the boat and tugged at a short ribbon under his collar, whereupon his overcape disappeared inside the main garment. He then pressed a button and the whole thing changed colour, consisting now of grey and red stripes. 'The bowler-hat is just as ingenious. Look: I press the band on it, and you can see it's black. Now I am properly dressed to go in for a consultation with his Grace the Bishop of Truro. I press a bit more, and – wait for it! – it's white. I'm going for a stroll in the castle woods, in summertime. I stop pressing and it's cream again, just the thing for travelling, because of the dust on the roads. And just look here inside: inkwell, pen, a clock made by Evans and signed and sealed by him. The clock is a great help, because in the Welsh lawcourts legal speeches are timed by an hourglass, and most of the barristers get distracted watching the drip of sand from the upper part into the lower, and lose the thread of their argument. Now whenever I invoke the king's name, or Magna Carta, I solemnly doff my hat and check the time while I'm at it. I've won a case or two with the aid of this little gadget.'

Felipe was much cheered by all these novelties, since it seemed he had returned to the good old days in Miranda, when he was page to Don Merlin and there were lots of visitors with strange and curious things. The traveller and the ferryman jumped ashore and tied up the boat. On May evenings in Pacios a low mist often forms, and the river runs silently across the fords. All you can hear is a little birdsong and some distant voices. The two men went up to the inn, and as they walked Felipe told the Englishman that they would find there a year-old Leonese wine, well-warmed and just the thing to suit the humours of the body in springtime. Mister Craven drank very slowly, filling his mouth with wine and swallowing it little by little, in the Gironde manner; he explained that in this way one avoids an excess of air in the stomach, because if air gets in there it emulsifies the wine and destroys its fine tilth, as it were, and its breadth of vision. Mister Craven found the wine most agreeable and not at all tasting of the wineskin.

'Since the railway got here', said the innkeeper, who was supervising the tasting of the new vintage, 'wine comes in casks.'

The Englishman opened his black leather briefcase, took a few papers out, moved his chair over to the window, and said to Felipe, 'I'm going to read a few odd bits of information to you, drawn from this book and that, plus some heard from Baron Galloden and others I've picked up on my travels, and all concerning the life and works of your former master Don Merlin the Magician of Brittonia. Most of them I gathered chasing across half Europe trying to trace the heirs of Baron Galloden. The problem is that in order to awaken the Baron's estate, currently fast asleep in the great bed of justice of His Majesty's courts in the city of Cardiff, I, the executor, have to present the complete list of legatees with their addresses. The only ones missing now are those who might have figured as twigs on Don Merlin's family tree, plus a few more who may descend from a granddaughter of the head psalm-singer of the Presbyterian Church, who left Scotland years ago with a cheap Italian camera and was last heard of as a widow in the Kingdom of Aragon, working in the rag trade and exchanging chamberpots and Talavera crockery for old clothes.'

Mister Craven took a reading-glass with a silver frame from his pocket, and after clearing his throat with two little coughs, began to read out, in a nasal tone with oratorical flourishes, the following:

Merlin's Birthplace

It seems that Merlin's birthplace was a clearing in the ancient forest of Dartmoor, in Greater Britain, out beyond the royal blacksmithery and not far from the Three Seats crossroads, these seats being those used by the fairies of ancient times when they rested and did their spinning, for threads of finest wool have been found on them. Merlin's first cradle was meadow grass, because there was no house or hut in the clearing, and his mother arrived at the spot as a fugitive, an unmarried girl who was pregnant by a button-seller who awoke love in her while she was standing at her window in an Irish town where her father held the post of fourth farrier to the king. You'll find the account of this love-affair in the Arthurian histories, in an incidental way, in the section that deals with famous makers of swords and their genealogies, though some set the matter aside under the title of:

The Tale of the Bearded Woman

This bearded woman was the only daughter of the fourth horse-shoer of King Donteach of Ireland. Her name was Scianabhan, which means 'jewel among women'. Her beard began to grow the moment she was christened. It grew thick and continuous, silky green hair on the left of her face, stiff red hair on the right. This was much admired: the blacksmith's house was visited by the monarchs when they went to their assemblies at Tara, and by very many people of all sorts, who were untiring in their praise of the bearded woman. She had grown up both well-mannered and witty, smiled politely at everybody, learned to play the harp, and was very skilled in the art of embroidery. But the beard was a bar to love. There was not a single prince, warrior, beggar, farmworker, or ferryman in all Ireland who ventured to ask for her hand in marriage, even knowing of her worthy attributes – her fine body, the sweetness of her gaze and of her voice, the beauty of her hands, and the wealth she would bring in her dowry – all because of the beard. Scianabhan would be twenty-nine next St David's day, and was beginning to mope. There was no question of removing the beard, for the more it was shaved off the greater the vigour with which it grew again, and in a few hours the face she had just rubbed with pumice-stone was as thickly afforested as ever. She no longer sang accompanying herself on the harp; rather, she and the harp wept as one.

None the less, love arrived. It happened that a youth by name Achy – that is, 'Red Neck' – passed by the smithy and spotted the bearded girl at her window, where she was sitting sewing a waistcoat for a tame nightingale she had (this evening woodland singer was an old bird now, and got ill in wintertime). The bearded girl answered the lad's salute cheerfully, and he went into the forge without further thought and asked a workman who was at the bellows if the girl was the famous daughter of the fourth blacksmith, and if she was still unmarried. Achy gave details about himself: that he had a mare named Bregia, a good breeder, in a field near Dublin, and two shares in a mill in Connaught, that he was a button-maker by trade, and so on, and right there in the presence of the blacksmith and his daughter, he took an ox-horn and made from it a complete set of buttons for a topcoat, each in the shape of a four-leaved clover. The fourth horse-shoer and his daughter found the lad much to their liking, and since he said he wanted to learn more about the character of his sweet intended before proceeding to marriage, they lodged him in the house.

The whole of Ireland was agog with talk of the bearded girl's love-affair, and the button-maker was happier each day to have found that jewel of a woman, and was already talking of getting married that Martinmas in Cork. Then it was that King Chluas Haistig – that means 'Flat Ear' – passed by on his way to attend a harp concert at Tara. He was one of the best-known among the 247 kings there were at the time in Ireland. Wishing to greet the happy couple, he went out after lunch into the countryside with the button-making lad and asked him how he had come to fall for the bearded girl and whether those colourful hairs were not an impediment to love. The young man answered, 'My lord, I fell in love with her when I saw her sitting at her window with her embroidery, since it seemed to me that she had a lovely face, with its left side reclining against a piece of green meadow which might have flown in through the air that morning, and when she turned towards me, to answer my greeting, I could see that she was blushing on the right side of her face.'

'So', insisted the king, 'you didn't realize that it was a two-tone beard?'

'Love did not give me enough time to study it closely, especially as I was listening to how her sweet voice came through the air to seek me out.'

King Chluas Haistig, who was the son of a witch of the same name, went that very night to see his mother, told her about his conversation with the enamoured button-maker, and asked if there was some remedy which could be applied to the beard of the daughter of the fourth horse-shoer. There was: it consisted in planting a sweet-pea seed in an ounce of woodland soil in the thickest part of the beard. As the pea-plant grew it would draw nourishment from the hair and the beard would diminish, to the point that when the plant came to flower, the beard would be altogether erased from the girl's face. Flat Ear sent this news together with a sweet-pea seed to the button-maker, wishing him love everlasting, a happy wedding, and abundant offspring.

However, it turned out that the medicine worked only if the girl applying it was still a virgin, and if she had been disobeying the sixth Commandment, the remedy would be so counterpro-ductive that her whole body would be covered in hair. Hardly had the pea taken root than hair began to sprout all over her person, and it was unpleasant hair, like that which cattle grow out on the hillside, and it was sweaty too. The button-maker was affrighted by such ugliness, and took off for France, where he looked for a job in Aix-la-Chapelle, in the robing-room of the Twelve Peers. Scianabhan was five months and a few days pregnant, and in order not to reveal her condition to the whole of Ireland, she passed secretly across to Greater Britain with a nursemaid, and there in Dartmoor Forest she gave birth to a son who, when he was christened, was named Merlin. At the time Galain the Lazy, grandfather of Arthur the Once and Future King, was ruling in both Greater and Little Britain.

Longwood School

When he was three years old Merlin went to Longwood School. This specialized in letters and arms, and there the lad studied Latin in Donatus and Greek according to the Alexandrian method, herbal remedies in Dioscorides, pharmacy in Galen, medicine in Hippocrates, pyrotechnics as systematized by Biringuccio, humours and vapours of the body according to Paracelsus, and alchemy as taught by Gabir the Arab. After five years he had solved the problem of the self-ventilating fireplace, which relies on the principle of squaring the circle as used in the craft of viastratology. Everyone was astounded to watch the young lad, already quite tall, with his bright eyes and his hair cut in mendicant friar style, debating with his teachers. Instead of going out to fly a kite or play leapfrog, Merlin spent his leisure time mastering Hebrew, the transmutation of metals, Homer, and the art of war. Soon after his eighth birthday he went off at his own wish to read medicine at Montpellier. The old nursemaid wrote off about this to the Gwirmoan ladies in Ireland – these were helpful fairies, who died in the great frost of 1627, the one they call the Gregorian Frost because it happened on St Gregory's day: the frost caught them while they were flying among the flowers in a garden belonging to a widowed Countess, trying to console her in her sad bereavement – and the three sisters sent water of the moon's waxing quarter in a sealed jar. On drinking just a couple of mouthfuls of this, Merlin turned into a youth of about twenty, with the beginnings of a golden beard, tall and elegant. Before leaving for Montpellier, Merlin went to the royal forge of Wales, to help in the making of the sword 'Plantata' for King Arthur, his role being to plunge the weapon in a secret liquid so that it should never rust. Owed also to him is the moat at Persse Castle, which consists of a channel of water on which floats a layer of soil no thicker than a finger, this sufficing to sustain a good deal of vegetation, so that no-one could imagine water lies beneath it: when enemy knights come charging boldly up they sink into what they assumed was the turf and flower-garden of everlasting summer. When Merlin was at work on these marvels he generally wore the double purple gown of university professors, and on the slightest pretext got his magnifying glasses out of their case when making some definitive statement, regularly larding this with some Greek or Latin axiom, ever keen to show off his knowledge of texts and branches of learning. At Persse Castle the old Countess had the young Breton princesses with her as ladies-in-waiting, and on Thursdays Merlin went up to the schoolroom to teach them Irish family trees and Carolingian heraldry, together with falconry, precious stones, and medicinal herbs. Among the little princesses there blossomed at the time the girl who would later be the wise Queen Guinevere.

'I'll leave out', said the Englishman, putting down his papers and wiping his reading-glass with his handkerchief, 'the youthful magician's period of residence and studies at Montpellier, and his trip to Ireland. He had his medical degree by then, and never took his graduate's cap and his yellow cape off that whole time. People came out into the streets in Cork to see him, and his marvellously hatted state caused confusion here and there. The beggars and children knelt down in the mud at the side of the Irish roads and especially by the bridges, asking him for alms, because they confused him with the Byzantine Roman Emperor, this Emperor having made it known (we have the learned Viviana's evidence about it) that he intended to go as a pilgrim to St Patrick's Well. Merlin managed to claim the estate of the fourth farrier, his bearded mother having died in a convent at Canterbury (to which she had retired as a harpist) of a coronary fluxion with complications, this necessitating a series of nine blood-lettings from which – they being administered under the sign of Pisces – the patient died. After that Merlin, following the advice of a Burgundian bishop who wanted to appoint him to his staff as head of household and confidential secretary, went off to Salamanca to read Scripture for two terms, whence he departed for Toledo to study Chaldean science, the Kabbala, and the astrolabe. About what happened in Toledo, I'll read you one account which is quite spectacular.'

Merlin in Toledo

Young Merlin decided to leave Madrid for Toledo. He was pretty confident about going there because, although it was stuffed full of daemons, learned Jews, witchcraft, and occult sciences, he had purchased the secret name of the city from Isaac Zifar in a hostelry in Medina del Campo: this Latin name is 'Fax', which means Firebrand, and it was made public quite recently. It's said that this Zifar fellow got rich selling this information to a lot of people, each of whom, thinking himself the sole possessor of the name, did not pass the information on. In Madrid Merlin had become friendly with a Neapolitan gentleman named Panfilo Atrisco dei Bottei, who had come to Spain in order to start an intrigue with the favourite of His Catholic Majesty – who at that time was the Duke of Lerma – directed against the Lord Viceroy of Naples. They met in the house of a Frenchwoman whose trade was dyeing walking-sticks, but there were girls there too, a merry crowd, who passed themselves off as nieces of the woman's late husband. The Neapolitan was perpetually astounded at Merlin's learning and particularly at his ability at encoding secret messages. Don Panfilo went in fear for his life, since he was sure he was being followed about by hired agents of the opposing party, and he asked Merlin if he would take letters he was carrying from Italy and deliver them by his own hand to the Duke of Lerma, who was spending the autumn in Toledo. The Italian would lend him as disguise a complete set of pedlar's equipment he had with him, including a stock of scented soap, rose-flavoured powders, and hairpins. Merlin agreed, attracted by the chance to approach the Favourite and get to know something of Spanish politics, and he liked the idea of going secretly into secret Toledo.

Just outside Illescas, Merlin was approached on the road by a good-looking dark woman, barefoot and bare-legged, who wanted to buy some jade ear-rings and a tablet of Alhama soap.

She paid with a silver coin, and as Merlin pocketed it he felt an urge to follow the dark girl in whichever direction she might lead, forgetting the important political message he was carrying, together with his status and noble learning, and even the post that awaited him in Burgundy. The girl took him to a hut, over towards the place they call El Viso de San Juan; on the way she told him that he had no option but to follow her, since he now had the Devil's coin in his pocket. She called him Don Panfilo, and talked bits of Italian to him: she was mistaking him, then, for the Atrisco man, and the spell would probably be a pretty minor affair. Inside the hut, sitting just by the door, was the Devil, writing away on a broad sheet of deckle-edged Barcelona paper. He had a big horn on the front of his head, and was using his tail to drive away the flies which were causing as much trouble as they usually do in Castile in the autumn.

The Devil, who did not give his name, greeted Merlin most courteously, calling him Don Panfilo de Atrisco. He said he was well aware of the Italian's high qualities, and said he had detained him only because he wanted to know what the Neapolitans call those little white cheese pies which they wrap in an egg batter and cook in frying-pans.

'They're called,' replied Merlin, aided at that moment by Don Panfilo's memory, '*mozzarella in carrozza, mozzarella* being the name of that delicate white cheese, almost cream.'

The Devil jotted the name on a corner of his sheet of paper, and after removing the silver coin from Merlin's pocket, instructed the girl to show the pretended pedlar to the Toledo road.

Merlin reached Toledo and in view of the nature of his mission put on his best clothes and went to deliver the secret letters to the Favourite. The Duke asked him how his journey had been, and Merlin told him about the Illescas incident. The Duke of Lerma opined that it had been some prank by humorously-inclined vagabonds, and laughed it off. He invited Merlin to join him next afternoon at his riverside villa, where his nephew was throwing a party. Immediately Merlin arrived the

Favourite drew him aside and asked him to say a paternoster for the soul of Don Giulio, Count of Güini, a Florentine who had been in the Duke's secret service, who had just died of poison in the Mesón del Francés in Madrid: the poison had been placed in *mozzarella in carrozza*, of which he was very fond.

Don Merlin had the chance to go to Italy, and sailed from Valencia to Ostia in great comfort, since it was June and the sea was calm. He made a purchase soon after arriving, and I give details of this and other matters in the story entitled . . .

The Journey to Rome

Don Merlin was waiting in the Los Galeros inn for his Pied-
montese mule – the one he had bought for his journey to Rome
– to be shod and returned to him. He was sitting under the
climbing vine enjoying the Italian morning and the blue sea and
day-dreaming a bit, with his eyes half-closed because the light
was so brilliant, when a beggar came up and asked for alms,
which Merlin gave him in his usual generous way. The poor
fellow was fat, lame, heavily bearded, and naked from the waist
up. His breeches, now ancient, were those of a Swiss Papal
Guard. He put his forefinger into one ear, revolved it, and drew
out a handsome gold ring with a fine ruby mounted on it, which
he offered to sell to the Magician of Brittonia for two of the
silver angels minted by the seaboard cities which he had spotted
in Merlin's pocket when he delved into this to give him alms.
Merlin thought the offer acceptable and closed the deal. The
beggar went off bowing away and saluting repeatedly by doffing
his cap, a shabby patched Spanish affair with which he covered
his unkempt hair. Don Merlin gazed long at the ruby, watching
the morning Mediterranean light play on each of its faces. When
he heard his mule's hoofs in the yard he wrapped the ring up in
a green silk handkerchief and tucked it away in a secret little
pocket in the neck of the short cape which he wore in the
summertime. This was the pocket in which he kept the code for
correspondence with King Arthur's Secretary for Celtic Letters,
and a pin steeped in poison of Caribbean water, which he had
bought in Toledo from a man newly come from the Indies. The
code used in the Arthurian Chancellery was the same which the
Laconians had used in ancient Greece, known in their tongue as
'skitale'. The Ephors had used it in their letters to ambassadors
and generals. The method involved a rod of olive-wood about a
span and a half in length, around which was obliquely wrapped
a bit of skin; on this the message was written, from top to

bottom, in such a way that when the skin was unrolled only detached letters appeared, and to read the message the recipient had to roll the skin again around a rod of the same dimensions.

Don Merlin reached Rome without further incident, well content with the calm swinging gait of the mule, whose name was 'Tirana'. He entered the city through the Porta San Paolo, pausing before he did so to see Caius Cestius' pyramid. He went along Via della Marmorata and crossed the Tiber by the Ponte Sublicio, looking for the San Michele hospice where he was to stay with a man who had been his companion at Montpellier, and who now practised medicine in handsome rooms he had in the house. This doctor was Master Orlandini. When a student at Montpellier he felt gloomy at times, leaning out of the window of his rooms, and if someone asked him what was wrong, he used to answer: 'I was dreaming of *carciofi alla giudia* and *spaghetti alla carretiera*, and washing it all down with a bottle of Marino, which to my taste is the best of the Castelli Romani wines.'

The first evening Don Merlin spent in Rome he had *ciriole coi piselli* for supper, dark Marino wine, and after spending an hour watching the light of the full moon on the fateful hills, he climbed into bed. He put out the light and then, just as his eyelids were starting to droop, saw a female figure dressed in airy green garments emerge from the secret pocket in his short cape. The apparition – for such it was – showed itself at the window for half an hour, and then returned very slowly to its hiding-place. The strange event was repeated on the three following nights, and since each night Merlin moved the ring wrapped in the green handkerchief (from which the female phantasm appeared) to a new place, Merlin concluded that he was the possessor of a magic ring. He hid the handkerchief under his pillow, whereupon the lovely finely-shaped figure, very sweetly scented, materialized beside his head, causing the fires of his lusts to blaze up a bit. On the fifth night Merlin resolved to banish unseemly thoughts by placing the ring in his secret pocket right next to the poisoned pin, and no ghost materialized. Next morning when he felt in the pocket to find the rod with the code so that he could write to King Arthur, he found it full of ashes, the gold of the ring turned to copper, and the ruby dead, changed into dull-looking glass. He put the ruby in the sunlight which was just coming up to gild the Palatine Hill across the river, and not a sparkle was to be seen in it. Master Orlandini and Don Merlin studied the case together, burrowing away in Cornelius Agrippa, Aristotle, and Dioscorides, and eventually came up with the answer: as the ghost materialized in the secret pocket she pricked herself on the poisoned pin, and since this Caribbean water is such a powerful poison, she died on the instant.

'It was a woman, and a very beautiful one', said Merlin. 'These ashes are full of love, I should think.'

He decided to go down to the river, and from the Sublicio bridge he tipped the ashes into the waters of the Tiber that were going down to the sea. Then he leaned on the parapet of the bridge and felt as melancholic as Master Orlandini had at his window in Montpellier when he yearned for artichokes done the Jewish way, and from his lips came lines of Latin poetry. The only one I can remember is this: *Sic te diva potens Cypri* ... which is by Horace. Merlin repeated it in Italian to Master Orlandini, and in English it goes: 'May the goddess who rules in Cyprus, and Helen's brothers, those two bright stars, and the father of all the gods, guide you.'

'I won't read the part about Merlin's return to Brittonia and the time he spent at the court of King Arthur, Once and Future King, because you can find all that in the history textbooks they read in school. Suffice it to say that the whole Round Table never had a firmer friend or a more diligent adviser, physician, or ambassador. One of Merlin's closest friends was the knight Don Lancelot of the Lake, who when he died was so warm in his praise of Queen Guinevere, the fact being that this Lancelot had a love-affair with Queen Guinevere behind the King's back, but people say it was one of those courtly affairs of the ancient kind that causes no dishonour.

'Well, I've read some things you didn't know about, and my throat's getting tired. I'll tell you just one more thing in conclusion. Don Merlin was in Paris studying lightning-conductors with Don Franklin when news reached him that he had property coming to him from an aunt, on his mother's side as most people think. That was in Galicia, where we are now. And since the man who was to become your master was more than a little tired of the rush of the world's affairs, and since the Revolution in France had left Lady Guinevere without the income she had derived from the whale-oil monopoly held by the Archbishop of Rennes in Brittany, and was asking Merlin for help, the two of them resolved to retire to Miranda and await better times. In Miranda they lived some sixty years in all, until Lady Guinevere, feeling her time had come, wanted to go and die in her native Wales, in a little orchard close to the ruins of Persse Castle, where she could listen to the skylarks and stroke the head of her old dog, black but a bit grizzled then by age, and nearly blind . . .'

'That was my Norés!' cried Felipe de Amancia. 'And was his backside white?'

The Englishman read from a note: 'It says here: "black, with white hindquarters".'

'It *was* my Norés! Ah, old fellow!'

The old boatman's eyes brimmed with tears. It was getting dark now. The turtle-doves were flying about looking for places to roost in the alders and willows along the riverbank. The moon was coming up over the Arneiro. The innkeeper lit a gas-bracket and called out to his daughter to come down and lay the table, since it was long past the Englishman's supper-time and he was hungry.

In Conclusion . . .

For me to try to make a full list of all the people who came to Miranda seeking help from Don Merlin's learning would be like trying to count the sands of the sea in one brief morning. When I started to set this account down I was not making any such list, merely trying to recall my own happy times, when this now ailing body was a vessel brimming with hopeful youth. Miranda is for me, as it was for each one who came and went through the gate there, not just a memory of the past, but an Easter egg or a clockwork snowball, like those which M'sieur Simplon was taking for the Bishop of Lamego to inspect. Days in the past, the clouds which shrouded some of them, thoughts which come and go, the very life itself which I feel within me, I could compare all of these with snow that comes drifting down, and as if providing a carpet for the earth covers farm plots and roads, meadows and threshing-floors, converting the face of the world we know into an immense level plain. But then there suddenly shines out the bright sun of some memory of youthful days, and it melts the snow in a few spots, just as if in a lonely world an unknown traveller should light a tiny fire, and you can go up to it and sit for an hour or two while you warm yourself with its heat. Ah, such memories!

Index of Proper Names

ALMEIDA, SENHOR – A Portuguese who accompanied the Greek mermaid known as Lady Theodora to Luiserne. He was a watchmaker of Chaves.

ALSIR, SIDI MOHAMMED IBN – A Tunisian Moor who travelled with a safeconduct from the Sublime Porte, selling compasses, essences, and history books. At the Tilsit fair he acquired the mirror of the Signoria of Venice, and sold it at Elsinore to Lady Ophelia. He gave Felipe de Amancia *The Tale of the Devil's Fart*, being the work of M'sieur Guy Tabarie.

ANGLOR, PRINCESS OF THE RHÔNE – who spent a year concealed in an umbrella belonging to a Canon of Avignon, dressed only in her blushes. The page François, nicknamed Pichegru, fell in love with her.

AQUITAINE – A province of France which lies to the right of the Pilgrims' Road, that is as you go from Lugo. A land famous for wine and easy women, if the proverb 'if the land is all sandy, the women will be all randy' is to be believed.

AUGUSTUS – One of the Roman Caesars who married Livia, who was five months pregnant by another.

AVALON – An island where Don Amadís de Gaula has lived since marrying Lady Oriana. It is one of the most ancient and illustrious parts of Brittonia, and its name means 'place of mystery'.

AVIGNON – City of the Popes in France, famous for its bridge. They drink there a wine called Châteauneuf du Pape: drink it in autumn and you will think you are putting on a light overcoat quilted with doves' down.

AVIGNON, THE CANON OF – The master of page-boy Pichegru. He loved drum music.

BEJARANO, DON JOVITO – Of Salamanca, a guerrilla fighter beside his compatriot Don Julián. A man quick to anger. The fun and games his spirited stallion had with the mares of Meira Abbey upset the lay-brother who looked after the stable.

BELIANÍS, DON – A famous hunter in the lands of León, and half-brother of the old Archpriest of Los Vados. He fought in Father Merino's group. He bought books about gunpowder from the Mussulman Elimas.

BELVÍS – a Castle two leagues from Miranda, where the dwarf with the straw hats was steward. The young Countesses of Folgar lived there, who had a special liking for cottage cheese and Parisian ribbons. They had a little Pekinese that Don Merlin taught to whistle an aubade.

BELVÍS, COUNT OF – The young Count of Belvís, who attended (with his feathered cap and dwarf to carry his train) the funeral of Merlin's aunt once removed, on his mother's side. He loved cards and playing the guitar, and died of excessive exposure to moonlight while he was in Granada serenading an apothecary's widow whose fancy he had been tickling.

BLACKSMITH'S WIFE, THE – Daughter of the eldest of the young lords of Humoso. The mother came to Pacios as a young girl, already married to the cobbler at Noste, and the heir of Humoso fell in love with her as soon as he saw her. The cobbler had no way of getting the young lord to leave Noste, and being a sensible chap, when Arximira – yes, that was her baptismal name – was born, he responded to the jokes of those who alluded to the horns the Humoso squire had placed on his head by remarking, 'Well, I either had to kill him or let him get on with it!'

BRAGA – City where the Primate of Portugal resides, and in which Lady Theodora, the Greek mermaid, buried her faithful Portuguese lover. At one time a famous electuary of oranges was made here, 'Braga hydromel', just the thing to cool down the livers of persons of saturnine temperament.

BRITTONIA – The country from which my mistress Lady Guinevere came. She had a palace there with two rose-bushes and a nightingale. It is a great kingdom that extends from sea to sea, but is now much divided, since its last ruler, King Arthur, was transformed into a crow during a battle.

CALIELA, LADY – Princess of Gazna, whose name is to be interpreted as 'liquid honey'. She beds Emperor Michaelos of Constantinople, with the intention of destroying his will-power; then causes him and his army to wander lost in the sands of the desert. She wears nothing more than a little golden bell on one knee.

CASILDA – A servant in our house, who had earlier been guide-girl to the blind man of Outes. She had a child by the umbrella-maker at Sebes.

CASTEL, MONSIEUR – A servant of His Grace the Bishop of Paris, who brought the parasols and paradarks to Miranda. He was fat and red-faced, with a fringed toupee which his lover, errand-girl for the Capuchin nuns in the rue des Lapins, used to curl for him. He had been promised a choir-stall with prebend among the canons of Sens Cathedral, but died of a surfeit of blackbirds cooked with onions before he could take minor orders.

CERÍS – A blind albino cat, which Lady Guinevere brought from Brittonia. The whiskers of these cats are much esteemed as aids to the removal of grains of sand that get into people's eyes.

CHALDEANS, CHALDEES – A subterranean people who, while hunting the serpent Smarís, discovered the beam of gold on which the mass of the world rests.

CHRISTOPHOROS – The polemarch or commander-in-chief of the Byzantines. He sent the courier Leonís to Miranda to ask Merlin for the Lay-it-down-pick-it-up-route.

COBILLON – A perfumier and well-perfumed daemon, a master-deceiver who tricked a widow of Soria with a fart which smelled of nard.

CORANTINES – A dwarfish, secretive people who live underground and devote themselves, according to Cornelius Agrippa, to guarding treasures. The Corantines disguise themselves as little dogs of the sort seen in Flemish paintings when they hold their festivities. They are said to have invented the still and use it to make truffle brandy.

CROIZÁS – A daemon from Pamplona, turned by Don Merlin into a bunch of blazing straws. He was of the fornicating persuasion. In Miranda he passed himself off as Don Silvestre, elected mayor of Bordeaux.

DAUGHTER OF LADY CAROLINE, THE – Her real name was never revealed. She went to Thule to study sewing and how to make almond sweets. She was a princess of the Chaldees and was betrothed to Don Paris. Miss Spindle keeps her prisoner, in the form of a pigeon when there is a procession.

DEAN OF SANTIAGO, THE REVEREND – He came to Miranda to buy some silver nutcrackers for the Chapter of the Holy Apostle.

DWARF – The dwarf of Belvís or of the Panama Hats. Nobody ever found out what his name was. He considered himself a gentleman and carried a sword. A perpetual story-monger and retailer of gossip in the great houses. Very prone to fall in love, he none the less died a bachelor. He had an obsession about bringing the telegraph line from Lugo to Belvís.

EDINBURGH, ST ANDREWS OF – A medical school, one of the most famous in Christendom, which used leeches *ad majores*.

ELEONORA, LADY – A niece of the Grand Inquisitor of Naples, who purchased the daemon-bathtub in Fossano.

ELIMAS – An Arab magician who earned his living selling secret books about the occult arts and telling tales in the inns. He was of the tribe of the Chaldeans.

ELSINORE – A castle in Denmark where the Moor Alsir had an audience with Prince Hamlet, and where Lady Ophelia lived. It stands close to the sea, and has a garden enclosed inside to protect it against the sea-winds.

ESMERALDINO, DON – The Cock of Portugal.

FELICES, DON – Formerly cantor of Santiago Cathedral. He told fortunes by cards. He came to Miranda to get his hourglass repaired.

FLORINDA, MISTRESS – The widow of Soria, who fell in love with the daemon Cobillon.

FLUTE, MASTER JOHN – Lord Sweet's personal flautist. He escorted the fragmentary remains of Lady Teardrop (may she rest in peace) to Miranda. He composed 'The Swan's Pavane', with words by the widow of the Anglican Bishop of Liverpool. He was very fond of *farinati*.

FOG, LADY – Second aunt of the monarchs of Thule, she lived in sin with a Frenchman who was chief ironer and starcher at Versailles. The French fleurs-de-lis came into Thulean heraldry through him.

FROILÁN, FAIR OF SAINT – The famous fair of Lugo, during which Felipe de Amancia saw, at the Teatro Ideal do Valenciano, the tragedy about Don Cruces.

GABIR, THE ARAB DON – Learned in secret books and alchemical science, under whom my master studied in Damascus.

GALLOWS, DOCTOR – English physician to the Khedive of Egypt.

GAUL – An island and kingdom way out in the ocean, from which Lord Amadís took the title of his crown. It is now a somewhat concealed part of the divided Empire of Brittonia.

GAZNA – City and Kingdom in the eastern part of the Byzantine Empire. Seven giant princes rule there, septuplet sons of a hunchback, and all married to Lady Caliela; they enjoy her company conjugally on a rota of one lunar month each, and then allow her one lunar month's rest, which she spends in a pool.

GIOVANNI DE TREVISO, DON – Of the family of the Dukes of Aragon, he was gonfalonier of the Holy Church. He was married to Lady Teardrop, and died a leper in Florence.

GUINEVERE, LADY – My mistress, former Queen of Brittonia. Most high, noble, and puissant lady.

HAIRY, MASTER – Physician from St Andrews of Edinburgh, who restored Lady Teardrop to life.

HAMLET, DON – Prince of Denmark, melancholic and dubitative, whose suspicions and cruel death are to be seen in the playhouses.

HUGUENOT OF RIOL, THE – A French phantasm who haunts

the manor-house at Riol, in Asturias. Abbé Laffite wished to take him off to Santiago de Compostela as a pilgrim in a phial of Murano crystal. He retained all his Protestant bile, as was seen in his reply to Jovito Bejarano.

LAFFITE, THE ABBÉ – A French cleric who went on pilgrimage to Compostela. He did not in the least resemble French abbés as they appear in novels. He specialized in castrating young turkeys for Christmas, and was much sought-after in Guyenne and Médoc to preach the sermon on the Descent from the Cross. As he came away from watching the bullfight at Vic-Fesenzac, he had a vision of the Archangel Michael.

LAMEGO, HIS GRACE THE BISHOP OF – The lame Bishop of Lamego. He had a barrel-organ and a crow that could speak Latin. He bought snowballs and musical-boxes from M'sieur Simplon. He did a version of the minutes of synodal meetings in Portuguese verse, and when he went on pastoral visits taught his clergy how to make mayonnaise.

LEONÍS – Page-boy to Emperor Michaelos. He emerged from the desert and came to Miranda to ask for the loan of the Lay-it-down-pick-it-up-route. He was one of the many in love with Lady Caliela.

LIAÑO, O – Innkeeper of Pacios. His hostelry was next to the mooring-rock used to tie up the ferry.

LUCEIRO – Our horse at Miranda. He was crossbred American, and had a long white tail.

LYONS – A French city with a famous fair. Some think the fair superior to those of Monterroso and at Mondoñedo around St Luke's day.

MACAREA, LADY – Princess of Constantinople, mistress of the elegant white mouse, the tip of whose tail was embellished with three black marks.

MANOELIÑA DE CALROS – A servant in our house. I taught her the art of spitting cherrystones, and I married her when they gave me the job of ferryman at Trigás.

MARCELINA, MISTRESS – Niece of the lawyer at Azúmara and head cook at Miranda. She used to fall regularly in love with any visitor. When Merlin left, she opened a restaurant at Lugo.

MARVELS – The name of one of the Bishop of Paris's umbrellas. His Grace uses it on Whit Sunday, and when he is under it has the gift of tongues.

MEIRA – Former Bernardine house, right next to the spring where the Miño river takes its rise. A famous town with a distinguished apothecary's which passed from the brethren to a lady of more than ample flesh, which she is said to have made freely available.

MERLIN – My lord and master. I do not say of him 'May he rest in peace' because we never heard that he had died.

MICHAELOS, THE EMPEROR DON – Chief Basileus of Constantinople. With his army he is lost in the sands of the desert, on account of the thirst-quenching charms of a princess of Gazna called Lady Caliela.

MONDOÑEDO – A city of Galicia, famous for its bishops and its horse-fair held around St Luke's day. Señor Cunqueiro, who put these stories into fair form, was born there. It is rich in grain, water, and Latin.

MONK OF GOÁS, THE SECULARIZED – His name was Don Ernestino, and he had been a Bernardine monk at Meira. He had a secret compartment in his shovel hat and kept a pistol in it. Originally from La Rioja, he sowed the whole glebeland of the church at Goás with Guinea peppers of the sort they call 'fire in your arse'.

MORNING STAR – One of the parasols which belonged to the Bishop of Paris. It dispersed darkness.

NAPOLI – The name of Merlin's double-barrelled shotgun, a present from the princeling of Palermo to my master. Merlin had cured his dog Perrís – who had a bull from the Pope which allowed him to point partridges at Castelgandolfo – of an attack of the farts.

NEPHEW OF O LIAÑO, THE – He went to the apothecary's at Meira to buy theriac and sedative honey pills for M'sieur Simplon. A trout-tickler of renown, he established the ferry at

Ansemar. At the time of his death he was a toll-collector at Lugo, having married a Portuguese girl who had worked in Madame Generosa's establishment.

NEY – One of our house-dogs, wolf-coloured.

NISTAL, ROMUALDO – A Leonese who kept a shop at Manzanal. He was a werewolf, and hanged himself in the Dueñas oakwood, as Elimas the Mussulman related.

NORÉS – Another house-dog at Miranda. He was black as night, and had been trained as an otter-hound. He was in the habit of sleeping in my room.

NOSSOLINI, MONSIGNOR DON PIERO – Grand Inquisitor of Naples. He exorcised from a bathtub the imp who wanted to watch the nuns as they bathed.

NOVAS, HIS EXCELLENCY – Portuguese companion of the Greek mermaid Lady Theodora. It is said that when he reached Luiserne with the lady, she was so sweet to him that he dived with her into the depths of the lake. He had a haberdashery shop in Mirandela, which passed to a niece who was married to a weaver who made ('By Appointment') white stockings for the young members of the House of Braganza.

OMEGA, DON – Chief watchmaker of Switzerland.

PABLO AND VIRGINIA – The names of two willow-trees on the bank of the Miño; they figure with these names in the inventory of property held by Don Merlin at Miranda in the province of Lugo.

PARIS – Paris, France, on the banks of the Seine, the city whose bishop had the parasols and paradarks. The daemon Cobillon has his perfume and scented-soap shop there. Its women are said to be as easy as ABC. This was where they unmanned Master Abelard for his affair with Heloïse; from the son the couple had, Astrolabius, there descend the Villiers de l'Isle-Adam, relatives of my master Merlin. The city is famous for its wealth and its deceits.

PARIS, DON – Prince of the dwarfish Chaldee people, hunters of the serpent Smarís, and betrothed to the daughter of Doña

Carolina, a prisoner in Thule. He proposed to turn the golden beam into coin.

PARSIFAL, LORD – A knight of Brittonia who went off to seek the Holy Grail, from a verse history which Lady Guinevere used to relate.

PAUL ET VIRGINIE – The novel by Bernardin de Saint-Pierre which made the little blonde Countess of Belvís cry when she was pregnant by the young squire of Belmonte.

PETRUS MUNIUS, DOMINUS – Abbot of Meira, in whose hood the Byzantine page-dwarf lived as a guest, when he came chasing after Lady Macarea's mouse.

RUFAS, AL HACH ISMAEL IBN SINA – Sheikh of the desert, poisoned when he sniffed a peach. He was a camel-castrator and owner of the magic carpet.

SCAREFLY, PRINCE – French musician, head ironer and starcher to the Court at Versailles, permanent companion of Lady Fog, Queen of Thule. He is the reason for the Thuleans having the fleurs-de-lis of France as their arms.

SEGOVIA – His Majesty King Charles VII's wolfhound, which followed the track of the werewolf in the woods of León.

SILVESTRE, DON – The shape which the daemon Croizás assumed when he came to Miranda with Doña Simona the enchanted.

SIMONA, LADY – Princess of Aquitaine over whom the daemon Croizás cast a spell. In Miranda she recovered her natural lovely form, and I shall never forget it.

SIMPLON, M'SIEUR – Former watchmaker to the Dukes of Savoy; he nearly expired in Pacios on his way with snowballs and musical boxes for the Bishop of Lamego.

SMARÍS – A serpent of Celtic origins, whose eggs have the power to turn the Chaldean dwarfs into a race of giants. It is said that Gargantua was weaned on a spoonful of meringue made from the white of one of these eggs.

SORIA – City of famous lineages, where lived the widow Florinda, whom the daemon Cobillon caused to fall in love with him.

SPINDLE, MISS – Regent of Thule. A capricious lady, who holds the daughter of Doña Carolina prisoner. Each of the Admirals of England has been to bed with her.

SUN-COME-OUT – Name of the Bishop of Paris's umbrella: when it is opened on the morning of the Assumption of Our Lady, even if it's raining, the sun comes out to light the world.

SWEET, LORD – Lord of the castle and region of Marduffe, in Greater Britain. He married Lady Teardrop.

TADEO – A moustachioed imp who came to Miranda as attendant of the daemon Croizás. He was hanged on the King of France's gallows in the town of Pons, accused of talking to chickens and shitting down people's chimneys. He had been apprenticed to a tailor in Toledo. He always paid his bills with Sevillian peso coins.

TARRAGONA – City in Catalonia, seat of the Primate of the Spains. It has excellent wines, and the daemon Cobillon claimed to have a town house there.

TEARDROP, LADY – A lovely silver creature, whom Master Hairy restored to life; she married Lord Sweet, but was smashed to pieces in a Roman garden.

TERMAR – A stopping-place on the pilgrims' road to Compostela, in lands belonging to the Royal Abbey of Meira. It is now called Feria del Catorce, and most of its inhabitants are Leonese and Sanabrians.

THEODORA, LADY – Greek mermaid, who came to Miranda to have her tail dyed in mourning colour for a Portuguese gentleman, her lover. She went off to become a nun in a convent deep in Lake Luiserne.

THULE – A hyperborean realm, the last land one finds beyond the Giant's Causeway. It produces lots of physicians. The daughter of Doña Carolina, who went to Thule to learn how to sew and make almond sweets, was held captive there.

TILSIT – A famous fair in Borussia, said to be twice as big as the Lyons fair and four times as big as the Monterroso fair. Nine different nations have the right to use their weights and their own interpreter there.

TRURO – City of the Princes of Cornubia, famous for the Deans of its cathedral. A niece of one of these had her hand turned to silver. Don Paris, Prince of the Chaldees, studied at the school there, lodging in the sleeve of the head subcantor. There are two woods nearby which have an abundance of nightingales, and the town is rich in springs.

TURPIN – A horse at Miranda, a light bay, exceptionally fast.

VERMEIL, MONSIEUR – Procurator of Calais, who had many dealings with mermaids, for whom he appeared in the Pont Mathilde Court in Rouen. He was very vain about his waistcoats.

WIDOW OF HIS GRACE THE BISHOP OF LIVERPOOL, THE – She wrote the words for Master Flute's 'The Swan's Pavane', and put the church calendar into verse each year for the use of the English. Her second marriage was to the coiffeur to the Court at St James's, an Italian who quickly left her when it turned out that she had false buttocks.

WINDSOR – Castle of the Kings of England, to which it was proposed to take Lady Teardrop to be married, and for her to be touched by the King, who was blind. It is a very windy place.

XAZMIN – Page-boy and stable-lad of the Lord Bishop of Paris, of whom Mistress Marcelina said that if she wished, he would return as her lover.

XOSÉ DO CAIRO – A servant in the household, a man much given to practical jokes, though serious too, and fearless. After Don Merlin's departure he stayed on as steward at Miranda, and married one of the young Belvís Countesses, the one with the reddest hair, who was pregnant by the young squire of Belmonte.

SUGGESTIONS FOR FURTHER READING

Very little has been published about Cunqueiro in English. Two essays by the present translator are in press: 'Alvaro Cunqueiro, 1911–81', to appear in a collection of papers of the Hispanic Research Seminar of the University of Oxford, edited by John Rutherford; and 'Alvaro Cunqueiro, Britain and Ireland', to appear in an issue of the *Bulletin of Hispanic Studies* (University of Liverpool). General studies in Galician include Anxo Tarrío Varela, *Alvaro Cunqueiro ou os disfraces da melancolía* (Vigo: Galaxia, 1989), and in Spanish Ana-Sofía Pérez-Bustamente, *Las siete vidas de Alvaro Cunqueiro* (Cadiz: Universidad de Cádiz, 1991); there is an already large bibliography in both these languages.

FOREIGN LITERATURE IN TRANSLATION
IN EVERYMAN

A Hero of Our Time
MIKHAIL LERMONTOV
*The Byronic adventures of
a Russian army officer*
£5.99

L'Assommoir
ÉMILE ZOLA
*One of the most successful novels
of the nineteenth century and one
of the most scandalous*
£6.99

Poor Folk and **The Gambler**
FYODOR DOSTOYEVSKY
*These two short works of doomed
passion are among Dostoyevsky's
quintessential best. Combination
unique to Everyman*
£4.99

Yevgeny Onegin
ALEXANDER PUSHKIN
*Pushkin's novel in verse is Russia's
best-loved literary work. It contains some of the loveliest Russian
poetry ever written*
£5.99

The Three-Cornered Hat
ANTONIO PEDRO DE ALARCÓN
*A rollicking farce and one of
the world's greatest masterpieces
of humour. Available only in
Everyman*
£4.99

Notes from Underground
and **A Confession**
FYODOR DOSTOYEVSKY *and*
LEV TOLSTOY
*Russia's greatest novelists ruthlessly
tackle the subject of their mid-life
crises. Combination unique to
Everyman*
£4.99

Selected Stories
ANTON CHEKHOV
edited and revised by Donald
Rayfield
*Masterpieces of compression and
precision. Selection unique to
Everyman*
£7.99

Selected Writings
VOLTAIRE
*A comprehensive edition of
Voltaire's best writings. Selection
unique to Everyman*
£6.99

Fontamara
IGNAZIO SILONE
*'A beautifully composed tragedy.
Fontamara is as fresh now, and as
moving, as it must have been when
first published.'* London Standard.
Available only in Everyman
£4.99

All books are available from your local bookshop or direct from:
Littlehampton Book Services Cash Sales, 14 Eldon Way, Lineside Estate,
Littlehampton, West Sussex BN17 7HE (*prices are subject to change*)

To order any of the books, please enclose a cheque (in sterling) made payable to
Littlehampton Book Services, or phone your order through with credit card details (Access,
Visa or Mastercard) on 01903 721596 (24 hour answering service) stating card number
and expiry date. (*Please add £1.25 for package and postage to the total of your order.*)

In the USA, for further information and a complete catalogue call 1-800-526-2778